CRIMINAL MINDS
FINISHING SCHOOL

CRIMINAL MINDS
FINISHING SCHOOL

A Novel by

Max Allan Collins

Based on the
CBS Television Series
Created by

Jeff Davis

AN OBSIDIAN MYSTERY

OBSIDIAN

Published by New American Library, a division of
Penguin Group (USA) Inc., 375 Hudson Street,
New York, New York 10014, USA
Penguin Group (Canada), 90 Eglinton Avenue East, Suite 700, Toronto,
Ontario M4P 2Y3, Canada (a division of Pearson Penguin Canada Inc.)
Penguin Books Ltd., 80 Strand, London WC2R 0RL, England
Penguin Ireland, 25 St. Stephen's Green, Dublin 2,
Ireland (a division of Penguin Books Ltd.)
Penguin Group (Australia), 250 Camberwell Road, Camberwell, Victoria 3124,
Australia (a division of Pearson Australia Group Pty. Ltd.)
Penguin Books India Pvt. Ltd., 11 Community Centre, Panchsheel Park,
New Delhi - 110 017, India
Penguin Group (NZ), 67 Apollo Drive, Rosedale, North Shore 0632,
New Zealand (a division of Pearson New Zealand Ltd.)
Penguin Books (South Africa) (Pty.) Ltd., 24 Sturdee Avenue,
Rosebank, Johannesburg 2196, South Africa

Penguin Books Ltd., Registered Offices:
80 Strand, London WC2R 0RL, England

First published by Obsidian, an imprint of New American Library,
a division of Penguin Group (USA) Inc.

First Printing, November 2008
10 9 8 7 6 5 4 3 2 1

I would like to acknowledge my assistant
on this work, co-plotter/researcher
Matthew V. Clemens.
Further acknowledgments appear
at the conclusion of this novel.

M.A.C.

For Brad Schwartz—
the Ness kid

PROLOGUE

Bemidji, Minnesota

The first rays of a November sunrise peeked over the horizon as if making sure the coast was clear before the sun gave up its cover. In his deer stand, fifteen feet up and wedged into a triangle of aspen trees, William Kwitcher looked down through the tightly bunched thicket, his breath visible.

A skinny man in his early thirties, Billy Kwitcher was covered head to toe in camouflage for the benefit of the deer that Daniel Abner, their guide, insisted would be here. One hundred yards to Billy's left, Abner occupied the next stand, and one hundred yards beyond Abner perched Billy's friend Logan Tweed. Abner, a balding man in his mid-forties, leased this land from Bassinko Industries, the lumber company that owned literally millions of acres of forest in the United States.

The guide had brought Billy and Tweed to this section of forest because gun season was now open, and Abner knew that the only gun hunters they might meet in these woods would be trespassers. Bow hunters would be in camouflage, while the gun hunters would be in orange. A camouflaged hunter moving around in a forest filled with gun hunters was just asking to be the victim of an accidental shooting.

Though he had practiced hard since last season, Billy was on only his second bow hunt. The first, last year, had proved dangerous chiefly to two pine trees Billy had plunked when he missed his meager two shots at bucks. He was better now, steadier. Working out had helped his strength, pulling the bow string, but had made no evident change to his wiry frame.

Below him, a six-point buck paused, nose in the air, sniffing carefully for signs of danger.

Holding his breath now, Billy willed the steam of his previous breath to dissipate before it reached the wary nostrils of his new target. Bow ready, arrow nocked, Billy tried to not move a single muscle as he waited for the buck to move farther toward the edge line separating the thicker growth that held his stand, and the thinner growth mere yards away.

Though the deer lived in the thicker woods, they fed in the nearby area, harvested about five years ago. In that section, the less dense trees allowed for more ground foliage for the deer to eat. That made the edge line, the border of the two areas, the place to hunt.

The edge line also made the buck more cautious than a field mouse trying to skirt around a sleeping rattlesnake. That was a sight not completely unfamiliar to Billy—once, back in the hills of his native Arkansas, he'd tossed a pebble at a rattler sunning itself on a flat rock. The snake coiled and its head popped up, its tail shaking its warning. A mouse on the nearby ground had frozen, in the vain hope that the snake would not see it. When the rodent finally made a dash for freedom, it got only two steps before the snake struck.

From then on, Billy had spent much more time studying snakes than mice.

"A hunter who can stalk a predator," his father had told him, "is a good hunter, indeed."

Billy Kwitcher had worked very hard at becoming a good hunter.

The buck beneath his deer stand sniffed the air again. Billy considered his options. From here, he had no shot. The only thing to do was wait. Finally, as if answering Billy's silent pleas, the buck took one step toward the edge line.

He sniffed; he stepped.

He sniffed; he stepped.

The tension was agonizing as Billy waited for the buck to give him an open shot. The passing seconds seemed interminable as the buck did its best to protect itself.

Finally, just as the buck edged into the harvested forest to feed, Billy drew back the stiff string of the bow, his muscles burning. He aimed, and just as the animal lowered his head to feed, Billy loosed the arrow.

He could barely make out the shaft's flight in the shadowy woods, but he heard the satisfying thunk as arrow met buck and passed through the creature before the deer even realized it had been hit.

As the arrow sailed off, the buck shuddered and stumbled, head popping up, eyes locking with Billy's for a split second before it turned away and sprinted off through the new woods, a red blossom visible just behind its shoulder.

When he saw that, Billy knew he'd made his shot. The arrow had pierced both lungs. The buck wouldn't die instantly, but the wound would be mortal.

That did not mean the carcass wouldn't end up half a mile or more away. Billy quelled the urge to climb down and take off in chase of the deer. One turn back this way by the buck could lead Billy right into the firing line of his two companions. That was assuming no other bow or gun hunters were in these woods. They weren't *supposed* to be, but Billy knew that phrase could end up being his epitaph. . . .

He checked his watch. The LED numbers read just after seven a.m. He was scheduled to meet the others at eight at the base of his stand. As the minutes crawled by, Billy checked his watch regularly, trying to will time to move faster.

Billy imagined different scenarios ranging from never finding the buck to poachers gutting his kill and leaving only the rendered carcass for him to find. None of his daydreams ended with him simply tracking down the buck, cleaning it, and hauling home all that meat. Such simply wasn't how Billy Kwitcher's life had worked out up till now.

Even the littlest success for Billy had to be tempered by some sort of serious setback. The unfairness of Billy's lot in life always seemed worse when Billy had time to think about it, and right now he had plenty of time to do just that.

At five until the hour, unable to hold off any longer, Billy sent a text message to his two companions. Right on schedule, Tweed and Abner appeared at the base of Billy's tree just as he got to the ground.

The three men stripped off their camouflage masks and all stretched to relieve the stiffness from being in the stands all morning. Under his mask, Abner—with a fire-hydrant frame and heavier than the others—had a scraggly gray beard, wire-frame glasses and stubbly patches of gray where his skull wasn't bald.

Still, it was Abner who moved easily through the woods. This was a point of contention with Billy, who wanted to be stealthy but usually had to settle for not clumsy.

Tweed had a hawkish nose, green eyes, and stood half a head taller than Billy. Around the same age as Billy, Tweed had an unruly mop of brown hair and a tiny soul patch that looked like dirt he'd missed when washing his face.

Tweed gave Billy a clap on the back. "Way to go! You got one, buddy."

Abner, the guide, gave him a thumbs-up. "Told you we'd bag a deer on this trip."

Tweed asked, "Was it a good shot?"

"Punched both damn lungs," Billy said, pulling himself up a little straighter.

"Cool," Tweed said. "Means he probably didn't get far."

But Abner was shaking his head. "You'd be sur-

prised how far a wounded buck can get. Suckers're
fast, and it takes a while for 'em to figure out
they're dead."

Billy led them to the spot in the edge line where
he'd nailed the buck.

Looking back toward Billy's stand, Tweed said,
"Damn good shot, Billy boy."

Nodding, Abner said, "Not bad. Not bad at all,
Billy." Kneeling, the guide looked at the blood spot
on the ground. "Frothy."

"Frothy?" Tweed asked.

Abner nodded. "Lung blood."

Billy wanted to stay cool, but his cheeks burned
pink with pride.

They all looked down at the scarlet puddle mixed
into the dead weeds and thin layer of snow. Last
night's flurries had left an accumulation of less than
half an inch. November in Minnesota meant always
straddling the possibilities of Indian summer or bliz-
zard conditions.

Abner asked, "Which way did it take off?"

Billy pointed southeast, back toward the road they
had come in on, where they'd left Abner's SUV. The
vehicle was a good mile or so away. Still, seemed
more likely the buck had veered into the heavier
woods and away from the road.

"All right," Abner said. "Let's spread out and find
the blood trail."

Tweed said, "Quite a bit of blood here. . . ."

"Some," Abner allowed. "But the drops will be

smaller and harder to see with the buck in flight. Stay sharp."

The trio spread out and slowly scanned the ground as they moved through the new growth of trees, in no rush. The forest, aspen trees, naturally grew back after a harvest, and that meant the lumber company did not have to plant new stems. Aspens were the backbone of the Minnesota lumber industry, their white trunks lining the two-lane highways that ran between many of the small towns up here, a good four hours north of Minneapolis.

Around them, the land rolled gently in easy hills, making the walk through the new growth fairly easy. Each man kept his eyes glued to the ground until one spotted a drop and would sing out, "Got one!"

They combed the terrain for half an hour. The trees in this part of the forest were barely taller than Billy himself and similarly scrawny, the bigger ones only slightly larger in diameter than the hunter's wrist.

No one had said anything for over five minutes, and Billy worried they'd lost track of the buck, and the hunter's stomach knotted as he worried they'd forfeited his prize.

Finally, he had done something right. *He*, Billy Kwitcher, had bagged a deer. Except the goddamned thing had disappeared, and Billy was beginning to wonder if he'd dreamt the whole damn thing. . . .

He bent lower, eyes flitting as he looked for any sign in the patchy snow or on any of the dead gray foliage.

Then his eyes started to burn and Billy had to bite his lip to keep from crying. Nothing had gone right for him since he had moved to this miserable frozen hell two and a half years ago. This deer hunt, this day, *finally* something had gone his way and now, goddamnit, it was turning to vapor. If the poachers he'd imagined earlier had gutted his kill, at least the carcass would be there, so he could have his buddies know that he had actually killed the damn buck. . . .

Now, he knew, they were both thinking that dumb ol' Billy had just winged the thing, then lied about his kill shot. More big talk, just like he always did down at Sully's Tap, Billy always wrapping his insecurities in braggadocio and, even as he knew he was doing it, powerless to stop himself. But this time, this one fricking time, he had actually done something worth *talking* about—except finding the proof was harder than nailing the buck in the *first* place. . . .

A glint of something red caught his eye.

He froze.

His eyes retraced their route and he saw it again: *a spot of blood.* They were still on the trail! He wanted to jump up and shout. He used his sleeve to swipe at his cheek, wiping away the tears. Of joy, this time.

Forcing himself to stay cool, Billy swallowed thickly. Next, he tried out his voice in a whisper, and it seemed to be working. He got up his nerve, took a deep breath and yelled, "Got a drop!"

"About damn time!" Tweed yelled back, already narrowing the distance between them.

From the other direction, Abner took a couple of tentative steps closer, then resumed moving forward.

Billy focused long and hard on the scarlet droplet, relishing the feeling of triumph he got from the dot of deer's blood. Then something on the ground next to the drop caught his attention, something sticking up and out of the snow and packed leaves, like a weird mushroom.

No, more like a *stick* . . . except it wasn't a stick— Billy knew that at once. Though the coloring was similar to the bleached bark of the aspen trees, he could tell it wasn't something from one of them.

This looked different.

Kneeling down, looking at the pale little cylinder, Billy realized that whatever it was, it had neighbors: two on the left and one on the right, pudgy little sticks similar to the first one.

Bones.

They were dirty and some of the surface had been scraped clean. Something had, he realized, gnawed the meat off. Stunned, Billy jumped back.

Abner called over, "What is it?"

"A hand!" Billy yelled back, as his two companions drew closer to see what all the fuss was about.

"What?" Abner asked.

"A hand, a goddamn *hand*!" For all its volume, Billy's voice was quavering, his eyes locked on the bony fingers that seemed to be trying to dig their way out of their isolated grave.

The other two pressed in close around Billy and looked down at his macabre discovery.

"Oooooh, shit," Tweed said, turning away.

"What the hell?" Abner asked. He looked at the fingers. "No goddamn way! This *can't* be happening *again*."

Billy blinked. "What can't be happening?"

Abner and Tweed shared a look, but Billy couldn't read it. The guide's face was as white as the bark on the surrounding aspens, and tears began to dribble down his cheeks. Neither man said a word, their silence speaking volumes to each other, but meaning nothing to Billy.

"*What* can't be happening again?" he repeated.

Tweed shot him a look. "Billy, just shut the hell up, okay? For once, just shut the hell up."

Billy began to respond anyway, but another sharp look from Tweed stopped him.

Not knowing what else to do, Billy sat down on a nearby fallen log and stared at the dead thing sticking out of the ground, as if waiting for the body to climb from the snowy ground and say something.

Tweed squatted and reached for what was left of the hand.

"Whoa up there, Logan," Abner said, pulling his cell phone out of a pocket. "You can't do whoever-it-is any good, at this late date. Best leave this for the cops."

Cops.

The word cut through Billy like the arrow he'd fired through the buck. Suddenly, breathing grew difficult, and despite the chill, he could feel sweat popping out on his brow.

Just like everything else in Billy Kwitcher's life, even shooting the buck was going to end up turning to crap.

Lewis Garue wore many hats: husband, father of two, member of the Red Lake Band of the Chippewa Nation, and today, detective—driving his own 2003 Toyota Land Cruiser in lieu of a Beltrami County Dodge Durango.

A deputy for nearly twenty-four years, and a detective for the last fifteen, the fifty-year-old Garue was stocky, his neck a short, efficient swivel for a block-sized head. His wavy black hair, worn much longer back on the rez as a kid, had gone mostly gray, and pouches had formed in his cheeks.

But any criminal who ran into Garue would testify that he was still a man not to be trifled with. After a four-year hitch in the Army, where he had been an MP, Garue attended Bemidji State University as a wrestler. He graduated with a degree in criminology and immediately got on as a deputy with Beltrami County. Married to Anna Yellow Hawk, his childhood sweetheart from the nearby Red Lake Indian Reservation, north of Bemidji (where they both grew up), Garue had settled into what was, for him, the ideal life.

The sun was still low in the southern sky, noon at least a couple of hours off. Garue's stomach was already growling. His wife always insisted he and their two kids start each morning with a "good, healthy" breakfast. Unfortunately for Garue, over the last twenty years, Anne's idea of a good, healthy breakfast had shifted from bacon, eggs, and pancakes to muesli, yogurt, and fresh fruit. Seemed like the detective was hungry all the time now.

He had been eating breakfast at home when he'd heard the dispatch call over his walkie. Three hunters had found something in Bassinko Industries forest number four, southeast of Bemidji. "Something" was as far as the description had gone. . . .

Now, two hours later, the call had come in that the deputies on-site wanted a detective. Sheriff Ewell Preston had naturally wanted his best investigator, and sent Garue.

The detective was supposed to be on comp time today, to make up for the overtime he'd put in on a series of meth lab raids over the last two weeks, but the discovery in the forest had changed that.

Though a plainclothes officer, Garue was not in his usual work attire of shirt and tie and sport coat. Well, the jeans were normal, but the rubber-soled black Rockys he wore on the job were replaced by boots, and his regular button-down shirt had been left on the hanger this morning, in favor of a Minnesota Vikings sweatshirt. Used to the just-above-freezing temperatures this time of year, he wore no coat.

Garue took U.S. 2 south out of Bemidji, then turned east on a county road leading to another two-lane running south through Bassinko's forest number four. The road was wet, the flurries from last night having melted off in this Indian summer day. Ahead, on the right, a service road cut back to the west, and

Garue saw three squad cars lined up on it; behind them was a van from the regional office of the Minnesota Bureau of Criminal Apprehension—the state crime lab.

As Garue pulled in, a deputy stepped forward to hold up a hand in "stop" fashion. Garue braked to a halt, then powered the window down as the deputy approached—a broad-shouldered blond kid, a rookie named Swenson.

The deputy smiled at Garue. "Sorry, sir—didn't recognize your car."

"Just doing your job," Garue said. "These are *my* wheels, son, no reason you should make 'em. . . . You first on the scene?"

"Yup," Swenson said with a nod. "Me and Sergeant Condon. He was right behind me."

"When did the crime lab get here?"

"About half an hour after us." Swenson checked his watch. "Make that a little over an hour ago."

"They find anything?"

Shrugging, Swenson said, "Dunno. I been out here. . . . Park on the side, would you, and you can just follow the crime scene tape. Should take you right to 'em."

"Thanks, son," Garue said.

The detective pulled in behind a squad car, climbed out and started tramping up the service road into the woods. He had gone maybe fifty yards when he saw crime scene tape wrapped around the trunk of an aspen.

The forest wasn't as thick here. This plot had been

harvested within the last ten years; the Bassinko outfit cut down plots of forty to eighty acres at a time, then allowed the plot to grow back over the next forty to sixty years before harvesting there again.

Looking deeper into the woods, Garue could see a strip of crime scene tape on another aspen ten yards on, then another, and another.

He was almost a quarter of a mile into the woods when he heard voices on the other side of a small hill. Over the short rise, Garue found a handful of men spread out in a semicircle, backs to him, and off to one side, three men in camouflage, obviously hunters, with a deputy. Those four men turned to see him as he approached.

The deputy, tall, rail-thin with hair as white as Garue's, wore no jacket despite the chilly morning. The tan shirt, with the three-tiered stripes of his rank, and brown uniform pants were freshly ironed, his shiny silver badge reflecting the sunlight.

Craig Condon was old enough, and certainly had enough time in, to retire. He hadn't, though. His wife was ill, and Condon needed the health insurance that came with the job, so he stayed on. Maybe longer than he should have, Garue thought.

Condon bestowed a solitary nod in the detective's direction—more greeting than he gave most people. The deputy's pinched face and long chin made him look serious, even on those rare occasions when the sergeant found something humorous. Today would not likely be one of those rare days.

Next to Condon stood the human cannonball that was Daniel Abner, and seeing Abner gave Garue a sick feeling, damn near a wave of nausea that had nothing to do with the breakfast his wife had served him.

Fifteen years ago, the disappearance of Abner's ten-year-old daughter, Amanda, had been among the first cases Garue had drawn as a detective. Garue and the entire Beltrami County Sheriff's Department, the Bemidji PD, and the regional state crime lab had worked ceaselessly for over a year before the little girl's body had been found buried in the crawl space of a house on the edge of town.

The house was owned by Abner himself, but had been rented to a former mental patient, Herbert Berryman, who had just up and left town about six months after Amanda's disappearance. No one, not even the federal boys, had ever tracked the man down.

Garue nodded toward Abner, but the guide, cigarette dangling absently, was staring into nowhere. Lewis Garue got the sense he wasn't going to like whatever these hunters had found here today.

The semicircle of men hovered around a device that looked like Rube Goldberg's idea of a push mower. Out front was a single tire that might have been appropriated from the BMX bike of Garue's twelve-year-old. A three-foot shaft ran back from the wheel and rode about a foot off the ground. A frame at the rear end attached atop the shaft, and within the frame were two boxes. Running up at an angle from the frame was a T-shaped handle. Garue had seen the contraption before—ground-penetrating radar.

The man running the machine was tall, broad-shouldered and in his mid-thirties—Fletcher Keegan. A graduate of the National Academy at Quantico, Fletch had been at the Bemidji office of the regional crime lab for the last four years. He and Garue were friends as tight as the aspens across the edge line of the forest.

Two of the other guys were also crime lab, though Garue didn't know their names. Two more were deputies, a kid whose name Garue had not learned yet, and Andy Salyard, a seven-year vet of the force.

When Keegan saw him, the crime scene tech waved, then shot Garue a no-rest-for-the-wicked glance, and went back to running his machine. Garue nodded to the rest, then joined Condon, who stepped away from the hunters to meet him.

"Bad day?" Garue asked Condon.

Nodding, the sergeant said, "Looks to be."

"Anybody talk to the hunters yet?"

"I did," Condon said.

"Which one found it?"

Jerking his head toward a scrawny-looking hunter, Condon said, "That one. Name's William Kwitcher. Billy."

Garue began his interviews with the guide, Daniel Abner. The bald man looked stricken. The murder of Abner's daughter had hit both parents hard. His wife, unable to cope with the loss of their only child, eventually divorced him and moved out of state. The guide had spent years getting his life back together.

Garue asked, "What did you see?"

Abner told about Kwitcher stumbling onto the skeletal hand. As the guide spoke, Garue couldn't help replaying in his mind the details of the Abner tragedy.

Tweed and Kwitcher echoed Abner's account. Everything seemed to check out, but something about Kwitcher's attitude bothered Garue. The skinny man seemed more nervous than shocked about his grisly discovery, but something else, too—scared? Guilty, even? Garue let it pass, for now; still, something about Kwitcher definitely got a blip going on the lawman's radar. When Garue finally let the trio go, however, Kwitcher was first to split. And the blipping increased. . . .

Fletcher Keegan came over to Garue and Condon. He took off his BCA ball cap, ran a hand through the brown stubble that passed for a haircut. Keegan had honest brown eyes, a square jaw, and wide shoulders—near as Garue could tell, an all-American guy.

"What?" Garue asked, in response to Keegan's frown.

"We've got ourselves a problem."

All the healthy food that Anna had fed him for breakfast felt like it might actually burn through his stomach lining. "What, don't tell me it's just the *hand*, nothing else?"

Shaking his head, Keegan said, "No, it's definitely a grave, all right."

"Okay," Garue said. "That's the bad news—what's the *really* bad news?"

Plucking his cell phone off his belt, Keegan said, "The GPR found three graves."

"Three?" echoed Garue.

"Oh yeah," Keegan said, punching some buttons on his phone. "Somebody made a personal cemetery out here."

Garue asked, "Who you calling?"

"FBI," Keegan said. The two men's eyes locked. "One of my guest instructors at the National Academy? He's with the BAU."

"The what?"

"Behavioral Analysis Unit."

"The profilers, you mean?"

"Yeah. Guy I'm calling is kind of the king of the profilers—maybe you heard of him."

"Yeah, who?"

"David Rossi."

"When we were children,"
Madeleine L'Engle said,
*"we used to think that when we were grown-up,
we would no longer be vulnerable.
But . . . to be alive is to be vulnerable."*

Chapter One

Quantico, Virginia

Jennifer Jareau studied the photos she'd just down-loaded to her laptop.

"JJ" to her friends and colleagues, the long-haired blonde in her late twenties had been with the Federal Bureau of Investigation's Behavioral Analysis Unit for the last five years, and had seen photos far more gruesome than these. But something about these victims—mostly skeletons now because of decomposition—engaged her interest.

Obviously, the three victims had been interred in their shallow graves near Bemidji, Minnesota, for some time. Exhumed over the weekend, the three bodies displayed levels of decomposition indicating burials over the course of at least several months.

She checked her watch, then printed the pictures and loaded them into a file folder with her notes as well as other documents from the investigators in Minnesota. She'd been accumulating information al-most since the moment Supervisory Special Agent David Rossi had phoned her to say a call would be coming from a Minnesota investigator named

Fletcher Keegan, apparently an old acquaintance of Rossi's.

Her fellow agent's heads-up had come so late that Keegan had called while Jareau was still on the line with Rossi. She spoke at length with Keegan, who in turn put her in touch with Detective Lewis Garue, lead investigator.

Of course, at this point, with the autopsies not done, the crime was the illegal disposition of bodies— a misdemeanor. But everyone on the Minnesota end felt they had a serial killer, and, judging by the strands of blond hair clinging to the skulls of the three corpses, that seemed likely; but the BAU could not get involved in a misdemeanor.

Her team, already in the office, was waiting for a briefing on what their next case would be, but first Jareau wanted confirmation on the causes of death.

Jareau was just about to inform her boss, Special Agent in Charge Aaron Hotchner, that the briefing would have to wait until after lunch, when the phone rang.

The call was from the Beltrami County coroner. Jareau spent half an hour taking down all the information and incorporating it into her briefing materials.

She called Hotchner and brought her boss up to speed.

"Don't rush yourself," Hotchner said. "We can schedule the briefing for after lunch."

"That would probably be better," she admitted.

Better if for no other reason than Jareau could keep

working through lunch, which today, like so many other days, would be at her desk. She had long since learned to eat without qualms while perusing the most grotesque write-ups and photographs of forensics evidence.

A PowerBar, a banana, and a container of yogurt from the break-room refrigerator kept her going as she prepared for the presentation. By the time she finished her lunch by downing a bottle of water, Jareau was ready.

When she entered the conference room, the others were already seated around the long, oval table. To the left, windows with venetian blinds let in November sunlight. A copier and fax machine on a sidebar shared the wall with the door. At the far end, a flat-screen monitor dominated.

Seated at the head of the table was team leader Aaron Hotchner, in an immaculate gray suit with a white shirt and striped tie—he might have been the CEO of a Fortune 500 company, not one of the top criminal profilers on the planet. His black hair was parted on the side, his well-carved face stern and businesslike, his eyes locked on the man to his right, David Rossi.

Fiftyish, with black hair showing signs of gray, Rossi was one of the originators of the BAU—along with the retired Max Ryan and Jason Gideon, he'd been among the unit's first superstars. After stepping down himself, then writing a series of true-crime best sellers, Rossi had made a small fortune on the lecture circuit before coming back to the BAU, in part to finish a case he'd walked away from. Today, Rossi wore a gray suit with a blue shirt and a tie with geometric shapes.

Next to Rossi, Derek Morgan, with his killer features and stylish stubbly beard, might have been a model for *GQ* and not a top federal agent. He wore a black mock turtleneck shirt with black slacks, and the only thing spoiling the male-model look was the nine-millimeter pistol holstered on his right hip. The son of an African-American police officer (killed in the line of duty) and a white mother, former college quarterback Morgan had spent time with the ATF, later serving as a hand-to-hand combat instructor here at Quantico.

Across the table from Morgan sat Dr. Spencer Reid, youngest member on the team. Reid had a distracted, little boy lost quality that endeared him to Jareau, the next youngest, and which belied the sharp focus he brought to every case, every moment. The lanky Reid had a mop of long hair, dressed like a prep school student, and was, judging by IQ scores, the smartest person in this or any room. With his eidetic memory, Reid seemed to have every fact in the world ready and waiting.

On Reid's right, SSA Emily Prentiss looked typically crisp in a sharp navy business suit, her black hair perfectly combed. Before the return of Rossi, she'd been the "newbie" on the team, but those days were over—Prentiss had long since proved herself a valuable addition. Tough and smart, with a sly, dry sense of humor, she was fitting in with the team on a personal level equally well.

No one said a word as Jareau set her materials down. They would wait patiently for her to start laying out facts. Once she did, however, well, the room would be far from quiet. . . .

Jareau centered herself, then began. "Saturday, three hunters in the woods outside Bemidji, Minnesota, found this."

She touched a button on her remote and the first photo appeared on the flat screen. This and subsequent images had been provided by the team's digital intelligence analyst, Penelope Garcia, who had used her considerable computer skills to enable Jareau to display images from her laptop onto the screen in the conference room. (Jareau couldn't have managed this feat herself, but she didn't have to—she, like everyone on the team, was just glad Garcia made all their jobs easier.)

The image was a stark, even grisly one: a skeletal hand sticking out of patchy snow and dead leaves, a small bloodstain nearby.

Reid was the first to interrupt, though there was nothing rude about it—give-and-take was normal here. "That hand," he said, eyes narrowed, "is far too decomposed to be the source for the blood on the ground."

Jareau nodded. "The blood is apparently from a wounded buck the hunters were tracking."

Reid nodded back.

Jareau continued: "The hunting guide used his cell to call 911. The Beltrami County Sheriff's Office responded with two squad cars. The county seat is Bemidji. . . ."

Hotchner said, "They have one of the state's two regional crime labs."

"That's right," Jareau said. "So investigators from the Minnesota Bureau of Criminal Apprehension were sent out as well."

The team sat quietly as Jareau switched to a photo that showed police tape outlining the burial site, the hand still visible near one edge. In the background were two more tape outlines.

"This is why they're asking for our help," Jareau said. "When they used ground-penetrating radar to find the parameters of the first grave, they found two more."

Morgan frowned. "Two more graves?"

"Total of three," Jareau confirmed. "Here's where it gets interesting—the coroner said they were not buried at the same time, but rather over the course of as much as a year."

She touched the button and the photo switched again. This one showed the three graves dug up, the bodies next to them each wrapped from head to toe in plastic. Though the shapes were vaguely human, there was no seeing through the plastic shrouds.

"Each of our three bodies is wrapped identically," Jareau said, but that was already evident. "The outer layer is a huge piece of plastic, a paint drop cloth of the sort available for a few dollars at any home improvement store or paint supply store in the United States."

No one said a word as she brought up the next photo. This one showed a victim without the layer of plastic, a blanket covering the victim from head to toe. This was not the original find, since the hand was not exposed.

"Under the plastic, each victim was wrapped in a blanket," Jareau said. "Then beneath that"—she switched to the next photo—"each victim wore a winter coat and beneath that"—the next photo came up on the screen—"they were all dressed in nice Sunday dresses that were pretty well protected from the elements by the plastic. Still, decomposition didn't leave us much."

Hotchner asked, "What *do* we know about the victims?"

"They're all females," Jareau said. "Girls, really. Each between the ages of twelve and fourteen, the coroner thinks."

"IDs?"

Shaking her head, Jareau said, "Not yet. If the girls are from Minnesota, they must have disappeared years ago—they don't match any recent missing girls from the area."

Hotchner asked, "What other avenues are we exploring to identify the victims? Garcia's on this, I assume?"

"All morning and right now. Beyond her efforts, the state crime lab is contacting nearby states and the coroner is going the DNA route. The county sheriff is even using volunteers to comb through 'missing kids' Web sites."

Reid's head was tilted like the old RCA Victor dog. "Do we know anything at all about the victims, other than age?"

"Caucasian, fair-haired," Jareau said. "They range in height from just under five feet to five-four."

With a frown of thought, Morgan asked, "Sexually abused?"

"Decomposition too far along to tell. Closest thing to a sexual component here is that tampons were found in two of the bodies."

No one said anything for a while.

Then Rossi asked, "Cause of death?"

"COD, too soon to tell," Jareau said. "They all appeared peaceful in the grave—no apparent signs of violence. The coroner's doing toxicology, but we won't have the results for at least a few days."

Looking at the screen through slitted eyes, Prentiss said carefully, "They were laid to rest as if by someone who wanted to protect them from the cold, wanted them to be . . . safe."

Rossi gave her a humorless smirk. "Possible— killers have killed to 'protect' often enough." He shrugged. "But it's just as likely that the killer's a police buff, who knows about fiber evidence and just doesn't want any clues left in his car."

"Wayne Williams," Reid said as if on autopilot. He didn't need to explicate—they all knew the Atlanta child killer from the eighties, one of the BAU's first big cases and a cornerstone of their reputation. Williams had been convicted with the help of both fiber evidence and the BAU's profiling skills.

Looking from team member to team member, Rossi said, "I know we don't have much to go on yet. And I also know we don't play favorites. But the forensics guy on this was a student of mine. I'd like it if we could help out. But I'll understand if we take a pass, at least till we have more."

"Three girls whose descriptions are nearly identical," Hotchner said, "buried in three nearly identical ways, in three adjacent graves. Anybody think this is a case we shouldn't be investigating?" He was greeted with silence as his eyes slowly scanned the room, landing on Jareau. "Call the sheriff in Bemidji," he told her. "Say we're on our way."

She nodded.

"Now," Hotchner began, "I don't mean to sound like a mother hen . . ."

"Then don't," Rossi said.

That earned a grin from Hotchner, a fairly rare occurrence. "Just the same—it's going to be cold. Pack appropriately. We're wheels up in two hours."

Bemidji, Minnesota

Between not leaving until late afternoon and the length of the flight, they didn't land in Bemidji until evening. The regional airport looked like a hundred other small-town airports, with little foot traffic inside, and when they went outside, the first thing everyone noticed was that mother-hen Hotchner had been right—the wind seemed to be blowing straight down from the North Pole.

As the team stood on the sidewalk with their breath pluming, Jareau was wondering where the hell their SUVs were. The vehicles were to be brought up by agents from the Minneapolis field office, which was admittedly over four hours from here, but the field office had received plenty of notice to get up here on time.

Jareau tugged the drawstrings on her parka tighter. The chill reminded her of early winters in the Pennsylvania town she grew up in. She was about to punch the number of her contact into her cell phone when two Beltrami County Sheriff's four-by-fours rolled up.

Stepping out of the driver's door of the lead vehicle was a tall, sinewy, middle-aged Native American. He had gray-white wavy hair, pouchy cheeks and a small bulge just above his waistline that said he probably didn't work out regularly. Still, as he approached, his gait was just short of a swagger and, even with the biting wind, he still wore only a flannel shirt and jeans—and had considerable presence.

A younger deputy, in uniform, got out of the other Durango and came around to the passenger side, but stayed with the vehicle.

The plainclothes officer walked up to the group, and stopped in front of Hotchner as if he'd known the agent for years. Most people, when confronting the team for the first time, approached Rossi as the leader, and before that, the assumption had usually been made about Jason Gideon—something about their age, Jareau figured. This man did not do that. He went like a heat-seeking missile to Hotchner.

"Detective Lewis Garue," the man said, extending his hand.

"Special Agent in Charge Aaron Hotchner," Hotch said, and they shook.

"Thanks for coming in," Garue said. "I know the facts are a little sketchy, but you took us serious and we appreciate it."

"That's our job," Hotchner said. "Let me introduce the team. . . ."

Garue stepped to his right, facing Rossi. "You're SSA David Rossi."

Rossi shook hands with the detective.

"Your reputation precedes you, Agent Rossi. I've read your books, seen you on TV. Thought you were a bigger man."

"I don't seem to be," Rossi said with a grin.

Morgan, hands on hips, was grinning, too. "So it's true—you do have fans."

"One or two," Rossi said.

Garue had half a smile going himself. "I'm gonna wanna book signed."

"We can make that happen. But let's find out who's burying bodies in your woods, first."

"Fine by me."

Hotchner made the rest of the introductions, ending with Prentiss, who asked, "Lewis Garue?" A smile tickled the corners of her mouth. "As in, Lew Garue?"

The detective nodded, straight-faced. None of the others were following.

The detective said, "But my parents *did* change the spelling."

Hotchner asked, "What am I missing?"

"A phonetic game," Garue said. "Agent Prentiss speaks French, obviously."

"She speaks a bunch of languages," Morgan said. "But how did you know she speaks French?"

"I'm a detective, son. Phonetically, 'Lew Garue' sounds very much like a French phrase—'loup-garou.' "

"Which means what?"

But Rossi answered: "Werewolf."

Garue chuckled. "Very good, Agent Rossi. A little favor my parents did for me—thought it would make me tougher."

"Must have worked," Rossi said. "You look like you can handle yourself."

"I'm still here," Garue said with a shrug.

Rossi seemed to like that response. Then he asked, "What band are you?"

"Bear clan of the Red Lake Band of the Chippewa Nation."

The two men stared at each other for a long moment and Jareau wondered what was going on.

Very softly, and evenly, Rossi said, "That wasn't us, you know."

Garue waved a dismissive hand. "There's still a lot of bad blood about the feds on the rez, but here in town? You guys will be welcomed as heroes."

"The rez?" Prentiss asked. "You mean, reservation?"

For once Rossi, not Reid, was spouting facts: "On March 21, 2005, Jeffrey Wiese, a troubled sixteen-year-old, killed his grandfather, the grandfather's girl-friend, then entered Red Lake High School and in three minutes fired off forty-five rounds. He killed five students, a teacher, and a security guard. He wandered the grounds of the school for another six or seven minutes and randomly wounded five more students before killing himself. Since the tragedy happened on the Red Lake Reservation, the FBI came in to investigate, and many people were unhappy with the way the case was handled. They thought the FBI overstepped."

"In some cases," Garue said mildly, "they did."

Rossi continued. "Some people thought the FBI was out to get the Chippewas, when Louis Jourdain—the son of Floyd 'Buck' Jourdain, Jr., the tribal chairman—was charged with conspiracy, because he knew about Wiese's plan and didn't tell anyone. Some believed the FBI was guilty of conspiracy, trying to get Jourdain out."

Garue and Rossi were again locked in a mutual stare. "Some did," the Native American said.

Hotchner was taking this in with narrowed eyes. "Are we going to have a problem here?"

Jareau was thinking, *Some fan . . .*

But Garue shook his head. "Not with me. When Keegan said he was going to call Agent Rossi, I was all for it. You federal guys and gals may not be much at Indian affairs, but you're a hell of a lot better at this sort of thing than we local cops are."

"Thanks for that much," Rossi said.

"There's some crazy shit going on around here, and we need your kind of help." Garue shrugged. "Anyway, I really do want a book or two signed."

The two men shared a respectful if guarded smile; then their stare-down concluded.

"We could get started," Hotchner said, looking around with frank irritation, "if we knew where our vehicles were."

Garue faced Hotchner. "That's why Deputy Swenson and I are here. Your SUVs are downtown, at the law enforcement center. Sheriff figured it would be easier for us to chauffeur you, some—just till you get the lay of the land."

"Considerate," Hotchner said. "Thank you."

Garue looked from face to face. "Any of you been to Bemidji before?"

They all shook their heads.

"We figured as much. Better you ride with us awhile."

No one argued the point.

With the help of Garue and Deputy Swenson, the team loaded their gear into the patrol vehicles. They split up as they got into the SUVs, Morgan, Prentiss, and Reid riding with Deputy Swenson while Hotchner, Rossi, and Jareau accompanied Detective Garue.

Hotchner sat up front with Garue while Jareau and Rossi shared the rear. Even though wire mesh separated front and back, the inside of the Durango was toasty warm—Jareau found that a soothing relief, after their windy entrance to what seemed to be the southernmost tip of the polar ice cap.

They had only gone fifty yards or so toward the airport's entrance when Garue said, "The building on the right there is the regional crime lab, a division of the Minnesota Bureau of Criminal Apprehension."

Rossi asked, "That's Keegan's office?"

"Yeah," Garue said.

The one-story glass-and-brick building was mostly dark, though Jareau could see some fluorescent lights on in the rear part of the lab.

"That's probably his light in the back," Garue was saying. "He's been working full tilt on this one since Saturday."

On the other side of the road, a two-story motel sat vacant, its windows boarded shut.

Rossi asked, "What happened there?"

"Northern Inn," Garue said. "Too many other choices—the land was sold for a new Ford dealership and the motel lost its lease."

From the airport, Garue turned left. On the right side of the road, a pine forest ended right before an overpass for Highway 71 north to International Falls, less than two hours away.

As they passed under the highway, someone might have thrown a switch—the landscape changed from rural forest to urban sprawl, strip malls, big box stores, restaurants, and gas stations lining the four-lane thoroughfare into town.

Hotchner asked, "How many people in Bemidji?"

"Almost fifteen thousand," Garue said. "Growing more every day. Nearly seven thousand students at Bemidji State University."

Jareau asked, "Crime problem at all?"

"Mostly petty stuff. Certainly nothing like what you folks are here for. Some burglaries and so on. The usual meth freaks you find anywhere. With poverty so high on the reservations, you get some B and Es, people trying to get by however they can."

Rossi said, "That was plural—'reservations'?"

Garue nodded, eyes on the road. "Three. I grew up on the Red Lake Reservation, north of here. The Leech Lake Reservation is to the east, the White Earth Reservation, west."

"Things are tough for them," Rossi said, not a question.

"Yeah," Garue agreed glumly. "The White Earth Band is doing the best, unemployment rate only twenty-five percent. At Leech Lake, it's over thirty, and nearly forty percent at Red Lake."

"That's a lot of people," Rossi said, "with a lot of time and not many worthwhile ways to fill it."

"Got that right," Garue said. He shook his head. "Desperation makes people do things they might not otherwise."

"This UnSub," Jareau said, thinking it time to steer the conversation back toward the case at hand, "seems to have done just what he wanted to with these girls."

Garue turned right onto Irvine Avenue and the

retail strip was left behind for rows of well-kept older homes, mostly two-story clapboards.

For a couple of blocks, their driver said nothing and they lapsed into silence.

Finally breaking it, Garue said, "You know, you do this job long enough, you think you've seen everything."

"Yeah," Hotchner said, years of experience coloring that single word.

"We had a case a few years ago," Garue said, "crazy bastard stabbed his wife thirteen times. Then went into the bedroom, woke his three-year-old and slit the kid's throat. Woke him *up* first—Jesus."

Despite the heater, a chill settled over the car's interior.

"When we got to the scene," Garue was saying, "Daddy had propped the dead kid on the counter so the corpse could 'watch' as he made cutlets out of Mommy with a meat cleaver."

No one said anything.

"That was bad enough. Thought I'd never see any crime scene that could get to me again." He grimaced. "But after what I saw in the woods the other day . . ."

Garue turned left onto Eighth Street. A parking lot spread out before them on their right and beyond that sat a cluster of matching buildings.

Rossi asked, "What did you see in the woods?"

Another block passed in silence before Garue turned right onto Minnesota Avenue.

Finally, Garue said, "They looked so peaceful lying there. The coats, the blankets, the plastic, they were prepared by someone who . . . who loved them."

No one said anything. On the right, Jareau saw the first of the matching redbrick buildings. This one had the legend COUNTY ADMINISTRATION over its entrance.

"In the end," Garue said, "it was the complete lack of violence at the scene that got to me most. The last grave was shallower than the first two. Like maybe the perp . . . what did you call him? The UnSub?"

"Yes," Hotchner said. "That's our shorthand for Unknown Subject."

Garue nodded. "It was almost like your UnSub was rushed that last time. Everything else was identical, except the depth of the third grave. Somehow, the critters got to it and they picked at the plastic, and picked the hand clean, too . . . but that was all they got."

Rossi said, "We came to the same conclusion, Detective—that the killer, or whoever buried the bodies for the killer, might've wanted to protect them."

"It was the peacefulness of the graves that shook me. This is one cool-as-a-cucumber character. You just take these kids out and bury 'em in the woods like a dead pet? You can do that, man, you got something a lot colder than ice water in your veins."

In the next block, on the left side, the redbrick building carried the legend BELTRAMI COUNTY JAIL AND JUDICIAL CENTER. Garue pulled up to the curb in front of the third matching building. Over the door, this one had the words LAW ENFORCEMENT CENTER.

Garue and Hotchner had to open the back doors

to let Rossi and Jareau out. Jareau looked over and saw two black SUVs in the parking lot with U.S. government plates.

"This is home," Garue said. "This building houses both the Beltrami County Sheriff's Office and the Bemidji PD."

Hotchner said, "Looks fairly new."

"Nineteen ninety-eight," Garue said. "All three buildings. The county decided to do it all at once and consolidate everything. Actually's made life easier."

Rossi asked, "Any closer on the cause of death?"

Garue shook his head. "Tomorrow, if we're lucky. The coroner had to send material off to the lab. You want to go in and get set up, or just wait for morning?"

A part of Jareau hoped that Hotchner would let them check into their hotel and catch one last good night's sleep, because she could anticipate what kind of hours were coming; but she knew better.

Predictably, Hotchner said, "We might as well get started right away."

Garue raised a finger. "One more thing, while I'm thinking about it—Bassinko Industries likes to consider itself a part of this community. So don't be surprised if they send someone around to talk. The bodies were found on Bassinko land, and that's the sort of press they don't want. I wouldn't be surprised if they send you a sort of . . . liaison. Or maybe envoy is more like it."

Hotchner nodded. "JJ here usually handles that kind of thing."

Jareau—who had dealt with cops, media, angry parents, and a thousand things worse than a company hack—said brightly, "I'll gladly meet with him or her."

Inside, the tiny lobby held a bulletproof-glass-enclosed cubicle with a door on either side. One was marked BEMIDJI PD, the other SHERIFF'S OFFICE. The uniformed policewoman behind the glass waved at Garue and pressed the button unlocking the latter door.

Only a couple officers were working at desks in the outer bull pen; the light was off in the sheriff's office and the chief deputy's. Garue led them into a conference room, flipped on the switch and fluorescent lights in the ceiling flickered to life.

"Let's get our equipment set up," Hotchner said, "make sure everything's ready for tomorrow—want you all to get a good night's sleep, and then tomorrow, we'll hit the ground running."

They all knew their jobs, and in less than an hour, the conference room resembled their own back at Quantico. A white board on one wall was filled with questions written by Rossi and Hotchner, Prentiss and Jareau had set up the laptops and established contact with Garcia to make sure their computer communications were up, Reid was using a bulletin board on another wall to display the crime scene photos. While they all did that, Morgan added equipment to what had already been provided in the SUVs.

Once Hotchner was satisfied, they climbed into

their Tahoes and followed Garue's Durango to a chain motel, a four-story building overlooking Lake Bemidji, the reason the town sprang up here in the first place.

In her room, after she'd unpacked, Jareau stared out across the black lake, four stories below, stars glinting off its choppy surface as windblown waves worked the water.

Beyond the far shore, she could see lights from the east side of town. Somewhere here, among all these peaceful houses with their glittery little lights and drawn curtains, lurked a killer.

The BAU team would get a good night's sleep, have breakfast, then begin the hunt.

Chapter Two

Bemidji, Minnesota

You could not work at the FBI without getting used to seeing a lot of white people.

Supervisory Special Agent Derek Morgan had long since grown accustomed to that. But the short time he had spent in Bemidji, Minnesota—at the sheriff's office, in the hotel lobby, and going for a five-mile run this morning—had convinced him that he now found himself in the whitest place on the planet.

And according to some Internet research he'd done on returning from his run, the town turned out to be nearly eighty-five percent white. The dominant minority, Native Americans (everyone around here called them Indians), made up another thirteen percent. That meant that only three percent of the population, or about 450 souls if Garue's census figures were right, were African-American, Latino, Jewish, Asian, Arabic or Klingon, for that matter. Certainly not the racial mix of Washington, D.C., or Chicago, where Morgan grew up. . . .

Up here, snow wasn't the only thing that seemed to be all white. On his trek through the aptly named

Paul Bunyan Park, the only individual of color he'd encountered was a statue of Babe the blue ox, standing next to a sculpture of the park's legendary lumberjack namesake.

To their credit, none of the people of Bemidji had been anything but nice to him, and none had given him so much as a second glance. In fact, while he'd been running through the park, just north of the motel, a few had even smiled and wished him good morning. Several had waved.

That, too, was certainly different from D.C. and Chicago—in parts of the Second City, "Good morning" was grounds to dump you in Lake Michigan. Particularly before a first cup of coffee.

After showering and getting dressed in a gray mock turtleneck and black slacks, Morgan had checked his pistol, put one in the pipe, clicked on the safety, then holstered the weapon. Wearing a light jacket over the pistol, he carried his parka with him. He had no idea when he would get back to his hotel room and its snug and comfy bed, so he took everything he might need with him.

Down in the lobby, he found everyone else already there. At one table, Prentiss sat working a crossword puzzle, a morning habit passed along by Jason Gideon, while Hotchner and Rossi sat together having coffee, the older agent nibbling at a bagel. At a separate table, Reid and JJ were each working on a light breakfast; for her, a banana, a bran muffin, and orange juice; for Reid, a bowl of cereal and juice.

They all gave Morgan a nod or a wave as he

passed on his way to the breakfast buffet. He grabbed a doughnut, a banana, two boiled eggs and a cup of coffee. He pulled out a chair and sat at the table with Reid and JJ.

"Did you get some sleep?" she asked.

He nodded. "Some." The two eggs and the banana disappeared almost instantly. The doughnut and coffee, he savored.

Looking over at Prentiss, he saw her shaking her head at him over the top of her crossword.

"What?" he asked, wondering if he had spilled something.

"Doughnuts?" she asked.

"What?" he repeated, wounded now. "It's only *one* doughnut."

She was shaking her head again, eyes wide. "How in God's name do you eat junk like that and stay in such good shape?"

Morgan grinned. "Maybe God just likes me . . . or maybe I got up this morning, did one hundred pushups, two hundred sit-ups, and ran five miles."

They were all looking at him now, and with more suspicion than their average suspect warranted.

"What?" Morgan asked again.

"I realize I'm a little older than you," Rossi said, lifting one eyebrow, "but I'm pretty sure I sprained something drying off after my shower this morning."

That drew a chuckle from everybody, Morgan included.

He popped the last of the doughnut in his mouth, chewed, swallowed, then took a deep, satisfying drink from his coffee. "Health food," he said. "You can't beat it."

"Gloat while you can," Rossi said. "Next thing you know, you'll be fifty, gaining two pounds from just being in the same room with a doughnut."

Prentiss joined in. "There ought to be ordinances against secondhand fat."

Morgan laughed along with the rest of them, but did decide to skip a second doughnut.

The town wasn't that big, so—even though his only trip through had been last night—Morgan had driven back to the police station this morning like a native. Soon the FBI agents were in the conference room of the Beltrami County Law Enforcement Center, Hotchner on the computer linkup with Garcia.

"Any progress?" Hotchner asked.

"Not yet, sir," Garcia answered.

The zaftig blonde with the black-framed glasses always seemed cheerful through the computer link. Morgan knew her chirpy attitude was in part a facade and a defense mechanism, as their digital intelligence analyst carried the weight of what the BAU team encountered as much as they did . . . if not more.

"Keep at it," Hotchner said. "COD and the victims' identities will give us a big step forward."

"I'm on it, sir," Garcia said, and was gone.

They turned to greet Detective Garue as the middle-aged Indian entered the room in jeans, an open-collar button-down blue work shirt and Rockys.

Hotchner asked, "Any news on the local front?"

Garue shook his head. "Nothing yet."

"All right," Hotchner said. His head swung toward the team. "Reid, I want you and Prentiss to work victimology. I know it's sketchy so far, but do your best. JJ, introduce yourself to the sheriff and the chief of police. Let's get them on our side."

Garue offered, "I can introduce her."

"No, thanks," Hotchner said. "I need you to go to the crime scene with Rossi and Morgan. You know this area and we don't, so they'll need someone to answer their questions."

Garue's shrug said, *Okay.*

As they were going out, Hotchner turned to Morgan and said, "Don't be a stranger."

Morgan nodded.

Both Rossi and Morgan grabbed their parkas and threw them into Garue's unmarked Durango. The detective drove south, back past their hotel, then out of town. Before long, the cityscape gave way to fewer clustered houses; then the two-lane highway was bordered only by the white-barked aspens.

The farther into the forest Garue drove, the more Morgan was struck that whoever had buried the three girls out here in the middle of godforsaken nowhere had to be either a local or someone who visited the place regularly. No one was going to be able to find the exact same spot on three separate occasions unless he or she knew the area extremely well.

Morgan asked, "Lot of traffic on this road?"

"Some," Garue said. "Mostly locals, but it runs into Highway Two, which goes east to the Leech

Lake Rez, and that runs into Seventy-one—the road south to Akeley and St. Cloud. So this stretch sees a share of traffic every day. Plus, the lumber trucks are going through here all day long."

Rossi asked, "What about at night?"

Garue shook his head. "Mostly a ghost town." He turned right onto a well-worn dirt road.

Rossi asked, "This is it?"

"We're getting there," Garue said. "This is the service road for Bassinko Industries forest number four."

"Bassinko," Morgan said. "You mentioned them last night—I've heard of them. They're huge."

With a nod, Garue said, "Own ninety percent of the forest in this area."

Rossi asked, "What were hunters doing in here, then?"

"People can lease land from the company for hunting."

Morgan frowned in thought. "Who has the lease for this part of the forest?"

"Daniel Abner. He hires himself out as a guide to pay his lease."

Rossi said, "We know that name, don't we?"

Another nod from Garue. "He's the one made the 911 call."

Rossi was staring out his window. "We'll need to speak with him, of course, and the hunters with him."

And another nod from Garue. "I'll set it up soon as we get back."

The detective braked the Durango to a stop. They all got out, and the two profilers got into their parkas. Morgan let his hood flop while Rossi cinched his up tight. To Morgan, the November air smelled clean and crisp, just as it had this morning, only out here in the forest, even more so.

Garue gestured vaguely. "We walk from here," he said.

They hiked five minutes or so into the woods until they came over a low rise, from which Morgan could see the crime scene tape that marked the three graves—all in a row—and (from where the agents stood) each seemed roughly equidistant.

Morgan asked, "All the graves were the same?"

"Pretty much," Garue said. "Each girl was buried with her head to the north."

Rossi's hands were on the hips of his parka. "Graves look pretty precise."

"He didn't use a tape measure," Garue said, "but for eyeballing it, yeah, I'd say pretty goddamn precise."

Morgan asked, "Was this spot marked in any way?"

Shaking his head, Garue said, "Not that we could find."

Rossi was squinting in the sunlight as he looked all around. "How the hell did he find this very spot three times? All this terrain looks the same."

"Not to someone who knows what he's looking for," Garue said. "Agent Rossi, you're pretty good with people."

"I like to think so."

"You don't even have to talk to them. You study them, their behavior, and even before you meet someone, you know them."

Rossi gave up a one-shoulder shrug. "To a point."

"That's the way this killer—your UnSub—that's how he is with trees. He studies them; he knows them." Garue sought out the eyes of each profiler, first Rossi, then Morgan. "Either of you fellas hunt?"

Morgan shook his head, but Rossi nodded.

"Ducks, pheasants, quail, I suppose?"

"Mostly," Rossi admitted, obviously a little perplexed. "How do you know that?"

The Native American detective granted his guests a grin. "Because, if you hunted deer, you'd be better in the woods."

Rossi grinned back. "Detective Garue, I'm not used to getting profiled myself."

"Well," Garue said, "let me take a shot at the UnSub, then."

Morgan said, "Be our guest."

"By all means," Rossi said.

"Let's start," Garue said, "with this: He knows his way around the forest."

"In this part of the world," Morgan said, "that doesn't narrow the suspect list much, does it?

"Sure it does," Garue said with a sharp, mirthless laugh. "Down to all the foresters, lumberjacks, and sylviculturists who work for Bassinko Industries or any other lumber company in the area, plus the state DNR guys and the Forest Service employees . . . or any deer hunter in the upper Midwest."

"DNR?" Morgan asked.

"Department of Natural Resources," Garue said. "They issue hunting and fishing licenses and take care of, what else, natural resources."

Morgan cocked his head. "What was that other term? Silver something?"

Garue said the word syllable by syllable as if to a child, though Morgan took no offense. "Syl-vi-cul-tur-ist—they're people who grow trees."

Morgan said, "I thought that was an arborist."

Garue shook his head. "Sylviculturists grow forest trees commercially."

"So we have a hell of a long list of suspects."

Rossi said, "Let's start to narrow that down, then."

Garue's eyes tightened. "How do we do that?"

"We start with what we know."

"Which is what?"

"We know the UnSub is someone familiar with the forest. Probably comfortable in any forest, but specifically *this* forest."

"Okay," Garue granted, "what else?"

Morgan's sigh was visible in the chill air. "The way in here is off the beaten path—not only does the UnSub know the forest, he knows the area. Probably a local."

Garue was shaking his head. "You really think so?"

The detective seemed to doubt anyone native to his community could be capable of crimes like these. Morgan didn't know where to start with how wrong *that* assumption was. . . .

Rossi said to the local cop, "Could you find this

place if you didn't live around here? Three separate times?''

Garue considered that. Then he said, ''I see your point, Agent Rossi, but I just can't imagine anybody in our little community would be capable—''

Rossi cut him off with an upraised palm; Morgan smiled to himself, as he automatically thought of the clichéd ''how'' the old movies gave to Indians.

''Just because you say hi to someone at the Sip N Go,'' Rossi was saying, ''or have a beer at the bar with them after work? That doesn't mean that person can't have a darker, secret side. You've been on the job long enough to know that.''

Now Garue issued a visible sigh. ''Yeah, yeah, you're right. I got kids—you try to tell yourself that no matter how much bad shit you see on the job, none of it can touch you, or them.''

''Only,'' Rossi said flatly, ''it can.''

Changing the subject, Morgan asked, ''How much farther do these woods go?''

Garue shrugged. ''Couple of miles, anyway.''

Morgan pointed. ''There's a little rise here, but if you look through those trees to our right, you can see a small piece of the service road.''

The others looked and nodded.

Garue thought about what Morgan had said, then shook his head again. ''I see your point, son, but it'd be harder than hell to see anybody way in here.''

''Granted, but not impossible,'' Morgan insisted. ''And if that's the case, if the UnSub is burying bodies, why not go deeper into the forest?''

"Maybe he didn't notice that little piece of service road," the detective said. "Maybe he lugged the body and got a little tired and figured this was far enough. Or, if he dug the grave before he brought the body, then it's all a moot point. 'Cause the process would be a hell of a lot quicker and less likely for somebody way the hell in the distance to notice."

Morgan said, "That could be true, but, remember— if he digs the grave on a separate visit, he's doubling the risk that someone will see him."

Garue's eyes were slits in the weathered face.

"I think Morgan's onto something," Rossi said. "They're buried here because our UnSub wasn't strong enough to get the bodies any farther. He took great care with how he packed the corpses, and took similar care with the graves and their placement from each other. So why would he be careless about where he places the secret cemetery?"

Morgan cut in: "And why would he increase his risk by making two trips for each body?"

Rossi continued, "Because if he predug the grave for one, it would make sense that he did it for all three. There's an almost ritualistic pattern to these burials. And not only does he risk being seen, he's risking someone finding the open grave. Way too iffy for a guy who's been this careful with everything else."

Garue looked at the tiny piece of the access road visible through the trees and thoughtfully said, "He's gone over a quarter of a mile, over uneven ground, carrying a body. He gets this far, he's worn out, and if he hasn't dug the grave ahead of time, he still needs to do that. If he goes any farther in, he risks not having the strength to dig the hole."

"Right," Morgan and Rossi said together.

"The holes are important too," Garue said. "The oldest two were deep, a hell of a lot deeper than I would bury something in the woods. He really didn't want these bodies found. The third one was shallower. Why?"

Rossi said, "Something spooked him, maybe."

Garue's eyes widened. "Hell. Do you think someone *saw* him?"

Shrugging, Morgan said, "Something must have made him nervous, or else why is that grave shallower than the other two?"

Garue shook his head glumly. "Finding what spooked him is going to be goddamn impossible. . . ."

"Not necessarily," Rossi said. "If we can determine when the bodies were buried, we can start figuring out what might have been the stressor that caused him to deviate from his pattern. Who would normally come in here?"

Garue thought about that. "This time of year, hunters. Also, the forester in charge of inspecting this area . . . although that can rotate, and there could be more than one forester in the picture. Hell, Bassinko has a bunch of foresters."

Rossi pressed. "Anybody else?"

"Some people might use the area for hiking in the summer, although, technically, they would be trespassing."

Morgan asked, "Why here?"

Garue frowned. "Pardon?"

"Why *this* place?" Morgan said, pointing at the ground. "Of all the places in and around town, why this *particular* place?"

"Random?" Garue asked with a shrug.

Shaking his head, Rossi said, "This is not a place of convenience. It's out of town, it's off the beaten path—no, he came here for a reason. If not convenience, then more likely it was comfort. The UnSub came here because, for some reason, he was *comfortable* here."

Morgan was looking all around them. "What's different about this part of this forest?"

After taking several moments to turn in a complete circle to study their surroundings and consider Morgan's question, Garue finally said, "Nothing. Nothing sets this part of the forest off from the rest of it. Of course, this *is* different than most of the forests in the area."

Rossi asked, "How's that?"

"You see how the trees are thinner here than that area over there?" Garue asked, gesturing toward where the three hunters' blinds were.

Both agents nodded.

"That's because this area has been harvested. Judging by the growth, I'd say about ten years ago."

Morgan asked, "Who would know that for sure?"

"And," Rossi added, "who would feel comfortable here because of that?"

Garue shrugged. "All the same people we've been

talking about—hunters, foresters, sylviculturists. Plus, most anybody who grew up around here knows the difference between harvested forests, and ones that haven't been cut down for a while."

Rossi twitched a frown. "We're going in circles."

Morgan studied their surroundings. "Tell me about the hunters."

Garue squinted at the profiler. "The ones who found the graves, you mean?"

"Yeah. Were they just walking around out here?"

"No. They were tracking a buck one of them shot with a bow."

Morgan considered that. "Deer are hunted from blinds, right?"

"Stands," Rossi corrected him.

"Yeah, but the hunter stays in one place and the deer come to them."

"That's right," Garue said. "They hunt the edge line, the area between harvested and unharvested forests. That's where the deer like to eat. You see this ground around us? Lots of different plants here. The trees aren't big enough to keep the sun out yet. When that happens, the smaller plants die off. These other plants are the deer's favorites, so they feed in the recently harvested areas. But since they're cautious animals, they live in the thicker woods . . . like over there. That's where the three hunters' stands are."

"If you knew these graves were here," Rossi said, "you could sit up there and see them?"

Garue shrugged. "Probably. If you had binoculars, easy."

Morgan asked, "When does hunting season start?"

"Gun season, last Saturday. Muzzle-loader season starts at the end of the month, and bow season has been going on since middle of September."

Rossi and Morgan traded a look.

"If the last body," Morgan said, "was buried in September or later . . ."

"Maybe *hunters* spooked our UnSub," Rossi said. "There might be a deer hunter out there who saw something and doesn't even know it."

"Oh, hell," Garue said. "There's a lot of bow hunters, but Daniel Abner leases this land from Bassinko. He would've probably led any hunters in here. We need to talk to him, more than before."

"Good place to start, anyway," Rossi said. "Let's get back to civilization."

On the drive in, Garue phoned into the office and asked that someone call Abner and have the guide come around to the law enforcement center.

When they got back to the conference room, Hotchner told the trio that a deputy had come in to say that Daniel Abner, the hunting guide, was already waiting in interview room one.

"Before you interview him," Garue said, "there's something you should know about Dan Abner."

"What's that?" Morgan asked.

"He had a ten-year-old daughter who was kidnapped, raped, and killed."

Hotchner stepped forward. "Why weren't we told about this right away?"

Garue looked perplexed. "I didn't see the relevance."

"A similar crime to this," Hotchner snapped, his temper showing through, "and you didn't see the relevance?"

"I'm telling you about it now," Garue said, keeping his cool. "It was fifteen years ago. Cost him a daughter and a marriage. He was never a suspect— well, not really anyway, no more than any family member is in such a situation—and the suspected killer disappeared before we could arrest him. In the fifteen years since, not one other girl has disappeared from the area. Abner's *not* your UnSub. He's another victim. Which is why I'm telling you this. He's got ghosts—we all do—but this is going to wake his."

Calmly, Hotchner said, "We need all the facts, that's all. You needn't worry—we'll handle him with care. Morgan, you do the interview."

"You got it, Hotch."

Garue led the parade to the interview room. He, Hotchner, and Rossi went into the observation booth next door while Morgan took a deep breath, then went on in.

The balding man at the table puffed on a cigarette, an ashtray handy. Evidently, Bemidji either didn't have a city ordinance against smoking in public buildings or someone had cut Abner some slack. Morgan guessed option number two.

Morgan smiled more to put the man at ease. Abner did not return the smile, but did nod.

"Mr. Abner, I'm Supervisory Special Agent Derek Morgan."

Abner nodded again, said nothing, and stamped out his cigarette in the ashtray. Morgan sat opposite the man, the two silently studying each other. Abner wore a flannel shirt, jeans and ankle-length boots; his mostly bald head bore patches of halfhearted gray the color of the stubble on his chin. Dull gray eyes lurked behind wire-frame glasses, and his expression seemed a little lost.

Still, Abner had not said a word and Morgan could only wonder if Garue had also left out the fact the hunting guide was mute.

"I'd like to talk to you," Morgan said evenly, "about what you found in the woods over the weekend."

Abner nodded.

"What did you find?"

Abner just sat for a long moment.

Morgan was fighting irritation when the man lit up another smoke and, finally, looked him in the eye.

"It was sickening," Abner said.

This, though something of a non sequitur, was at least an answer. Morgan prompted, "Sickening?"

Abner sighed smoke, nodded. "In one goddamn second, I went from having a fun time with some buddies to knowing exactly what the guy who found my daughter must've felt like. Man, I thought I was going to puke, made me so sick to my stomach."

"We were told about your daughter," Morgan said. "I'm very sorry for your loss."

Abner said, "It was a long time ago. But . . ." He shrugged, sighed smoke again. "It's not the kind of thing you get over, really."

"I know it's difficult, sir, but I need to hear your story."

The guide thought for a moment. Morgan was about to prompt him again, when he said, "I was hired by Billy Kwitcher and Logan Tweed to take them on a deer hunt."

"Both locals?"

He nodded. "I've known Logan all his life. He was almost ten years behind me in school, but I knew his older brothers."

"What about Kwitcher?"

"Him, I don't really know that well. Just a friend of Logan's. Him and Logan went deer hunting last year, with another guide."

"Do you know what guide? Would you have a name for him?"

"Nope. Sorry."

"Do you know anything at all about Kwitcher?"

"I'm pretty sure he works construction with Logan."

"Not a lifetime Bemidji resident?"

"Naw. Billy told me he moved here a couple of years ago from . . ." Abner shook his head. "All I can remember is somewhere down South. Arkansas, Missouri, Oklahoma, something like that."

"All right," Morgan said, never having heard a more vague rendering of Southern states. "Tell me the rest of the story. I'll try not to interrupt."

Ten minutes later, his face ashen, the pain of his own daughter's disappearance obvious there, Abner wrapped up his account.

Morgan leaned forward. "You had no idea that anyone had been in the forest?"

Abner shrugged. "I can't go that far, Agent Morgan. There's no way to keep people out—not to mention that Bassinko folks are in and out of there, now and then. After all, they own the land, what's to stop 'em? If I went in there and saw new tire tracks? I wouldn't think a thing of it."

Morgan mulled this for a moment before asking the next question. If he asked all three hunters the same question, perhaps the three answers together would provide the team with something helpful. This was important; an adage gleaned from their evidence-gathering colleagues said, *First on the scene, first suspects.*

"You've told me how you reacted to finding the skeletal hand," Morgan said. "Now I'd like your impression of Kwitcher's reactions, and Logan's."

"Their reactions?" Abner said, almost sputtering. "The same as mine! We were all freaked out as hell. Jesus, what do you think?"

Holding up both hands, Morgan said, "Whoa, slow down a little."

Abner ground out his cigarette and immediately started up another.

"You were all surprised," Morgan said. "Granted. Think about it for a few seconds . . . then tell me what they were doing while you were making the 911 call on your cell."

The hunting guide puffed away on his cigarette as if the act of inhaling fueled new thoughts.

"They were both pretty worked up," Abner said, at last. "In different ways, though. You're right, when I think about it, all our reactions were at least a little different."

"How so?"

"Like I said, it made me sick to my stomach. All those memories . . . but the others, well . . ."

"Yes?"

Abner met Morgan's eyes. "Logan was . . . I'd call it . . . *curious*, you know?"

"I'm not sure I get that."

The guide tried again: "He almost reached out and *touched* the thing a couple of times." Abner shuddered. "I mean, I had to *stop* him. It was like he wanted to hold those bony fingers. I don't know, maybe he thought . . . Shit, I don't *know* what he thought. But I had to tell him the cops wouldn't want the scene disturbed, or I swear he would've touched that hand. Hell, he might even have pulled it out of the ground! Like a goddamn flower he was plucking."

"And Kwitcher?"

Sighing smoke again, Abner said, "His reaction was somewhere between Logan's and mine. Billy stayed away from the hand, but let me tell you—he couldn't stop staring at it. The weird thing, though?"

"Yeah?"

"When I looked in Billy's eyes, it was like he was . . . somewhere else. He was staring at the hand, but he wasn't really seeing it. He was looking *through* it. Seeing something else. It was like he'd just seen a damn ghost or something."

Morgan nodded. He scooted the chair out and stood. "I don't have any more questions for you, sir. Thank you for your time."

"Glad to help."

"We may need to talk again. This can be a long process. So don't be alarmed if you hear from us."

"Okay." Then, his eyes burning into Morgan's, he said, "You find this son of a bitch, you give me five minutes with him alone, and save yourself the cost of a trial."

From the look in the guide's eyes, Morgan knew the man spoke the truth.

"I understand the sentiment," Morgan said with a grim little smile. "But you might in future want to keep thoughts like that to yourself."

Back in the conference room, Hotchner gathered the group around and filled them in on the interview.

Morgan said, "Well, Abner's big enough to have moved the bodies."

Detective Garue said, "You consider him a suspect?"

Hotchner said, "We consider everyone connected with the crimes to be at least a person of interest . . . until they're not."

Reid asked, "Was he serious about that threat he made?"

Morgan nodded. "If it's an act, it's a damn good

one. He had me convinced that if he and the UnSub are left alone together . . . the UnSub won't walk away."

Prentiss, eyes tight, asked, "Could he be covering his tracks? Talking big to make us look somewhere else?"

"Possible, of course," Morgan said with a shrug. "My gut is to believe him . . . but on the other hand, no one in this town would ever question Dan Abner's vehicle being on that forest service road."

Garue looked stricken. "I can't believe you're considering Dan," the local lawman said. "After what he's been through? When does a guy get cut a break from you people?"

"When he or she is no longer a person of interest," Hotchner said, voice calm. "Look at the profile that's emerging. Abner's comfortable in that forest. He knows it as well as or better than anyone. No one would question his being there. He's had major stressors in his life, with the loss of his daughter and his wife leaving him. When was the crime?"

Garue said, "I told you, fifteen years ago."

"No—what month, what time of year?"

The detective had to think, but he finally said, "She disappeared in April. Found her body the following June."

"When did his wife leave him?"

Garue thought some more. "September of the next year, I think it was 1993."

"So," Reid said, "two months ago was the fifteenth anniversary."

"Guys," Garcia said from the speakers and screen of a laptop.

Morgan turned and saw the curly-haired blonde smiling at him from the monitor.

"Hey, girl," Morgan said.

She kept their usual jokey flirtation to a minimum with Hotchner and Rossi standing on either side of Morgan. "Hi, everybody," she said. "I finally got a background on your hunter, Billy Kwitcher."

"Good," Hotchner said. "By your high standards, that took a while."

"Well," Garcia said, "William R. Kwitcher only showed up on the radar two years ago."

Garue asked, "Where was he before that?"

"Living in Arkansas as William K. Rohl."

Hotchner asked, "You're sure it's the same guy?"

"Mr. Kwitcher's middle name is Rohl and Mr. Rohl's middle name was Kwitcher, when he fell off the world two years ago. Not surprisingly, they also share the same birthday."

"He changed his name," Rossi said. "Any idea why?"

The normally upbeat Garcia's expression was solemn. "Until he disappeared just over two years ago, William Kwitcher Rohl was a registered sex offender in Arkansas."

This news turned the room silent as suddenly and utterly as if Garcia had hit the MUTE button on her end.

The detective, Garue, found his voice first. "Sex offender, huh?"

Morgan said, "Abner said he looked like he had seen a ghost—no wonder."

Not even waiting for Garcia to fill in the details, Garue said, "We're going to want to talk to him. I'll bring him in, no problem."

The detective was already heading out the door when Hotchner said, "Morgan, Prentiss! Go with him."

They both followed Garue out the door, Morgan thinking that if Kwitcher had been spooked before, that would be nothing compared to how Billy would feel seeing the fire in Detective Garue's eyes.

Chapter Three

Bemidji, Minnesota

SSA Derek Morgan, SSA Prentiss, and the local detective left the conference room to bring in Billy Kwitcher, aka Rohl. JJ was with the sheriff, while Rossi and Hotchner were poring over reports from the case.

In the meantime, Dr. Spencer Reid sat at his laptop computer, looking at the image on the screen—the pretty, ever-pleasant face of digital intelligence analyst Penelope Garcia.

"Can you tell me anything about William Kwitcher," Reid asked, "before Morgan and Garue get back with him?"

Garcia's eyes shifted to another monitor as she read. "William Kwitcher Rohl, Billy, was arrested on two counts of sexual assault, which is of course a class A felony, on January 23, 2003. In August of the same year, he pled guilty to sexual indecency with a child—a class D felony. Served two years at the Tucker Unit of the Arkansas Department of Corrections—that's twenty-five miles outside of Pine Bluff. When he got out, in 2005, he registered with the state as a sex offender, then before long fell off the grid."

Reid asked, "Do you have the details of the crime?"

Garcia read silently for a moment, then looked at Reid. "Seems that Billy Rohl—Kwitcher is his mother's maiden name—had a threesome with two young ladies he met at a Pine Bluff convenience store. Plying them with cheap beer was apparently his method of operation."

Reid already knew where this was headed, but he waited for Garcia to say it.

"Both girls were fourteen."

The young profiler had been at this long enough not to be outraged or even shocked, though he wasn't proud of that. "Anything else?"

"Well, our boy Billy is in violation for leaving Arkansas without informing the state he was moving to Minnesota. Likewise, he's in violation in Minnesota for not registering with the local PD when he became a resident."

"No wonder he was nervous when he was questioned at the scene," Reid said. "What can you tell me about the two girls in Arkansas?"

"Understandably, their parents tried to keep this quiet. The girls didn't have spotless records themselves—underage drinking already on the books. That's why nobody complained when Rohl pled to a lesser charge."

"That makes sense," Reid said. "But, of course, you've dug deeper."

Garcia grinned and pretended embarrassment. "Why, Dr. Reid, you're paying attention."

Reid smiled back at her shyly. He realized Morgan would have had some witty comeback, or some flirtatious remark, but that wasn't his way.

"Both girls were blonde," she said. "Like your Minnesota victims."

Now Reid was frowning. "Maybe he's escalating."

"And it's probably already occurred to you that they were in about the same age range as your victims."

Nodding, Reid said, "Kwitcher, or rather Rohl, isn't a very large man. From what Morgan has said, our UnSub probably isn't physically imposing."

"The girls in Arkansas seemed to have been party types; nothing like force was involved."

"True. And that might be the case here in Minnesota. It's not the sex that requires force—it's possibly panicking or even premeditatively deciding to clean up after the fact. The girls 'party' willingly, but wind up murder victims after."

Garcia was tilting her head. "The autopsy reports came in on the three girls."

"What have we got?"

"Cause of death was opiate poisoning. Insects tested from the decomposed bodies contained high amounts of codeine and thebaine."

"Hydrocodone," Reid said, eyes tightening. "Prescription pain reliever."

"That's right. The girls just went to sleep and never woke up."

"Nonviolent," Reid said. "Another sign that this UnSub loved his victims."

" 'Loved'?" Garcia asked, obviously uncomfortable with the characterization.

"In his own special way. This goes along with his method of disposal, dressing them up, the coats, wrapping them in blankets and sheets of plastic. In some way, he thinks he's protecting them."

Garcia shook her head, her distaste obvious but unspoken. "Still nothing on identification of the girls. I'll let you know as soon as I have something."

"Thanks," Reid said. "I'll tell Hotch."

Garcia disappeared and Reid went to tell their boss about what he had learned. But already he was having his doubts about Kwitcher—a guy who picked up underage party girls at convenience stores could hardly work up "love" for them, as reflected by the UnSub's ritualistic burials.

Or were these girls representative in Kwitcher's mind of some single lost love from his past?

Emily Prentiss felt a shiver run up her spine, but whether from fear or just the cold, she could not say. She certainly had on enough clothes—over her sweater she wore a Kevlar vest, and over that a navy blue Windbreaker with FBI emblazoned in yellow, front and back. Her Glock was in her hand, safety off, arm extended down along her leg keeping the pistol partially hidden.

Though the sun shone brightly, a biting wind had started ripping through from the north as she made her way into the teeth of it, walking carefully up the alley behind a two-story clapboard house on Twelfth Street NW, mere blocks from two parks and both Bemidji's middle and high schools.

As another shiver spread through her, Prentiss considered that the cold she felt might be neither fear nor wind, but the sheer creepiness of a known sexual predator having settled down here in Homespun, U.S.A., in the midst of such fertile pickings.

She settled in at the corner of the house's garage. Around her, the neighborhood was made up of similar houses, some in need of paint as much as Kwitcher's, most in better shape. The garages lined the alley like teeth on either side, a molar missing here and there where a door stood open.

Out front, Morgan and Garue would be preparing to mount the front porch steps, operating on the assumption Prentiss had the back covered, which she did. From her position behind the detached garage, using it for cover as she peeked around the corner, she could easily see the back door and most of the backyard.

In her earpiece, Morgan said, "We're approaching the front door and knocking."

Though she knew Morgan respected her as an agent, he would, occasionally, shift into the stereotypical male protective mode. That was why the two men had sent her to the back. She didn't resent this, exactly, realizing Morgan had far more experience going through doors; but this wasn't her first time on the street—she'd spent years as a field agent before joining the BAU.

Mildly preoccupied with that thought, she was startled, just a little, when the back door swung out like a slapping hand and a skinny man, probably about her size, dashed out into the backyard, face masked with fear.

"Rabbit on the run," Morgan's voice said in the earpiece.

No shit.

"Got him," Prentiss said into the cuff mike, and as that hand went down, the one holding the gun came up, and she stepped around the corner of the garage right into the path of their rabbit.

"Freeze, FBI!" she said, her pistol's front sight locked on the man's chest.

He was either deaf or stupid, and just kept coming, arms pumping as he sprinted toward her, determination replacing fear on his face, though the eyes were wild. No weapon was apparent and she wasn't about to kill him for panicking and running. . . .

The rabbit must have sensed that because instead of veering off, he plowed right into her, knocking her backward, the air whooshing out of her as she hit the earth, the gun tumbling from her hand in a lazy arc. But the suspect got tangled with her, and toppled onto her, a second impact that sent a starburst through her brain.

Prentiss fought through the pain and disorientation as she and the suspect both tried to scramble to their feet and away from each other's grasp. They were both wobbly and she launched a spinning kick that missed her target, the suspect's face, but landed squarely in his upper chest, knocking him back onto his ass again. By the time he started to rise, she had retrieved her pistol and held it inches from his frightened face.

"I think you ruined my pants," she said, her voice flat, but an eyebrow arched. "So I'm in *no* mood . . ."

Rubbing his chest, the suspect slumped back to the ground.

"On your stomach—spread-eagle."

He hesitated.

"What did I say about my mood?" she asked, her voice much sharper now.

He complied.

Morgan and Garue came tearing around either side of the house, each with his gun drawn. Then they slowed, seeing the tableau with Prentiss in command.

"Nice job," Morgan said with a relieved grin.

"Yeah, thanks," Prentiss said. "Next time, *I'll* take the front."

The squatting Morgan cuffed the suspect's hands behind him. "You're William Kwitcher?"

Still on his stomach, the suspect swallowed and said, "Yeah."

Morgan tapped him on the head, just a tiny but unmistakable thump. "Didn't your mother ever teach you not to run away from a federal officer?"

As they helped the suspect to his feet, Garue read

Kwitcher his rights. They led him to Garue's Durango and put him in back. The detective would drive him to the law enforcement center with Morgan and Prentiss trailing.

Fifteen minutes later, they brought Kwitcher in through the LEC's back door. Hotchner, Rossi, and Reid were waiting for them—JJ was in a meeting with the Bemidji police chief.

Kwitcher was deposited in an interview room. Prentiss, Morgan, and Garue watched from the observation booth as Rossi came in to interrogate Kwitcher.

The skinny man, his hands cuffed through a loop in the table, sat disconsolately, head bowed as Rossi stared him down.

Finally, Rossi took the seat opposite and said, "William R. Kwitcher?"

Kwitcher looked up.

"Or maybe I should say William K. Rohl?"

"Aw, shit," Rohl mumbled, shook his head, then looked down again.

"I'll just make it 'Billy,' if you don't mind. Because you're one rose that by any name is not smelling sweet."

The suspect lifted his eyes and gave Rossi a sulky look. "I didn't do anything. I found a body and we reported it. Like good citizens. So why am I in trouble?"

"I wonder." Rossi flashed a grin that had no amusement in it whatsoever. "Maybe it's because you're a registered sex offender in Arkansas, who moved away without notifying the state. Maybe it's because you're living in Minnesota where you, a sex offender, have *not* registered."

Rohl found a blemish on the table that seemed to him very interesting and studied it intently.

"Billy, you had sex with two fourteen-year-old blonde girls."

"They were willing. I didn't know they was underage. How are you supposed to tell these days? You seen how they dress, how they act."

Rossi ignored that. "Now you turn up at a deer stand overlooking the graves of three blonde girls of about the same age as your previous victims. Coincidence?"

"Those two girls weren't no victims," Rohl said indignantly. "That them girls buried out there was young and blonde, well . . . you're right. It's a coincidence."

Shaking his head, Rossi said, "Do you believe in God, Billy?"

"Sure I do."

"So do I. But I'm an atheist about one thing."

"Huh?"

"I don't believe in coincidence."

The suspect swallowed, shook his head. His eyes finally stopped avoiding Rossi's. "How can I prove to you I didn't do this thing?"

Rossi shrugged. "Gonna be tough. You *do* match the profile."

"Profile?"

With a gesture to himself, Rossi said, "That's why

the FBI is in town. We're profiling the killer . . . which, I'm afraid to say, is starting to look a whole lot like you."

Rohl's eyes flared. "I didn't do *shit*, I tell ya!"

Ignoring that, Rossi said, "The first thing we know for sure about the perpetrator is that he's a pedophile."

"Don't you call me that. I ain't no damned child molester. Them girls in that convenience store? They looked of age. They was buying beer, wasn't they?"

"Billy, do you think I didn't read the file? That's how you connected with those girls—*you* bought beer for them. And invited yourself to the party . . . party of three, I should say."

"You make it sound sick."

Rossi did a double take. "Billy, you had sex with two fourteen-year-olds. Even in Arkansas, that's pedophilia. And you're a statutory rapist who skipped and avoided registering as a sex offender. Yeah, I'd call that sick."

"You never saw them two girls. You'da thought they was old enough, too. I was just a normal man with normal needs."

"Have you ever had a real relationship with a woman twenty-one or over?"

"Hell yes!"

"I don't mean just getting laid, Billy—I mean a genuine, long-term, loving relationship." He leaned on the table. "I have a hundred dollars that says you can't give me the name of one woman who'll admit to dating you even three times, let alone having a relationship."

Rohl folded his arms and sulked some more.

"Thought as much," Rossi said. "Let's get back to the profile. You're not very big. Neither is the perp. He would've carried the bodies farther from the road, if he'd been able. On the other hand, maybe the graves were placed there so you could see them from your deer stand."

Rohl started to look frightened. "Look, you can be disgusted all you want about me and them teenage girls. But this isn't that—I'm a lover, not a killer. I didn't *do* it, man!"

"You ran."

"I was scared."

"Ran, and in the process, assaulted a federal officer."

"I didn't *mean* to! Christ, she kicked *my* ass!"

Rossi managed not to smile at that. "That what you're going to tell the judge, Billy? 'I was trying to escape, Your Honor, but when I knocked that female FBI agent down to get away, I didn't mean to, and anyway, she hurt me back'? I'm sure that'll play. I'd go with that."

Rohl lapsed into silence.

"You own a gun, Billy?"

The suspect eyed Rossi with distrust.

"Look, Billy, we're getting a search warrant for your house. We'll have it in fifteen minutes, and half an hour from now, we'll know. Why don't you score a point here and cooperate?"

He shrugged, looked away. "My grandpa's shot-gun's in the bedroom closet. It's a family gun."

Rossi nodded. "Thank you for cooperating. But you're now a felon in possession of a firearm, 'family gun' or not, and you've assaulted a federal officer."

"How was I supposed to know she was a federal officer?"

"Maybe the big yellow FBI letters on her jacket?"

The suspect couldn't find a reply for that.

Rossi continued: "Those are the federal charges so far. We'll also be looking into how much trouble you're in for leaving Arkansas without notice, and living in Minnesota without registering. Bottom line, Billy—you're going to jail. Your detention hearing will be tomorrow."

"I want to lawyer up."

"I would, too, Billy, if I were in as much trouble as you."

While Garue got Rohl booked, the others went back to the conference room. Prentiss plopped into a chair, as she rubbed absently at the mud stain on her right knee. She hoped it would come out—at least the fabric had held up.

Rossi poured himself a cup of coffee while Reid and Morgan found places at the table on either side of Prentiss. Hotchner went to the head of the table and sat. Rossi was just pulling out a chair to join them when JJ entered, holding several sheets of paper.

She said, "Judge just faxed the search warrant."

Hotchner asked, "Who's going to serve it?"

JJ said, "The sheriff's sending Detective Garue, the police chief's providing one of his guys, and I told them we'd have someone go along as well."

"Good," Hotchner said. Turning to Morgan, he said, "You and Rossi up for that?"

"Sure," Morgan said.

Both agents rose and headed for the door, Morgan taking the warrant from JJ as he passed.

Then, still in the doorway, the slim blonde said to the rest of them, "We have another issue."

"What's that?" Hotchner asked.

"There was only a small piece in the local Sunday paper. But a longer article ran yesterday, and that went statewide. Now the wire services have the story and it'll go national. The PD and the sheriff's office both have phones ringing off the hook."

"From the media?" Reid asked.

"Some of it is," JJ said. "Most of the calls are every other law enforcement branch in the country trying to figure out if one of the girls is from their jurisdiction."

Hotchner said, "That's not a bad thing, though there may be a lot to sort through. Are we getting leads from those calls?"

"As you say, we'll have to sort them out, but there could be. I'm going to help the locals set up a hotline." She sighed and smiled the smile of someone resolved to take on a major task. "We'll get this under control before the end of the day."

"Good," Hotchner said.

JJ nodded good-bye and was gone.

Getting more comfortable in his chair, Hotchner said to Reid and Prentiss, "Let's go over what we know so far."

"Three dead girls," Reid said. "Ages twelve to fifteen, victims of barbiturate overdose."

"All buried in the same area of the woods," Prentiss said. "Wrapped in plastic, blankets, a coat, and each had on what were probably nice clothes before decomposition. Interesting thing about the clothes—no tags."

"Torn out?" Hotchner asked.

"Could be," Prentiss said. "They could be homemade, too. The clothes seem nice. That might be a tip to the UnSub's economic level."

"Middle class?"

"Possibly," Prentiss said. "And, remember, it would take gas to get out there three times—nobody lives nearby. The clothes, the plastic, the blankets, that all costs money. Even the blankets were reasonably nice. It's not like he got them at Goodwill."

"Tags on those?"

"Removed as well, but it's certain that the blankets weren't homemade."

Hotchner asked, "What about abuse to the girls?"

Reid shrugged. "The bodies were too decomposed for us to know."

They all knew that signs of abuse faded quickly once decomposition began.

"According to the autopsy protocols," Prentiss said, "the victims all seemed well cared for, well nourished. With none of the girls having been abducted from the area, I begin to wonder if this UnSub didn't keep them with him for a while."

"That's worth looking into," Hotchner said. "How are we doing with identifying the victims?"

Reid said, "We haven't heard from Garcia on that yet."

Hotchner said, "Probably time to check in with her again. Emily?"

"Right away," Prentiss said.

Hotchner's expression was grim even for this fairly humorless man. "Something's not right," he said. "Rohl fits some of the aspects of the profile, but not others. He's certainly not middle class and doesn't seem to have a lot of money. So how do we explain the nice clothes?"

"They would cost less," Reid said, "if they were homemade."

"Yes, but does that mean Rohl has those skills . . . or did he have someone do it for him? And if so, isn't that an expense itself? He doesn't have a spouse or significant other."

An interruption came by way of a knock on the frame of the conference room door. They all turned and Prentiss found herself looking at a squat, spherical man with a scraggly beard and short, patchy gray hair on a balding skull. He wore glasses that seemed almost molded into a puffy nose, and carried a plastic ice cream bucket with a lid on it.

Hotchner gave their guest a curious but not unfriendly glance. "Mr. Abner?"

"Yes. I haven't really met anybody but Agent Morgan, and I can see he isn't here. But I wanted to say hello."

Hotchner said, "Well, that's fine, Mr. Abner. Let me make the introductions," and he did. The hunting guide shook everybody's hand, then returned to his position near the door.

Hotchner, with no particular grace, asked, "May we help you?"

To Prentiss the subtext was: *What the hell are you doing here, anyway?*

Abner gave them a half smile and took a tentative step in. "I think what you people are doing is really fine, and I just wanted to bring you this as a token, you know, of my thanks." He held out the plastic bucket, taking off the lid.

Reluctantly, Hotchner accepted both the bucket and the lid.

"It's cookies," Abner said as if Hotch had suddenly gone blind.

"Well, thank you," Hotchner said.

The aroma of the freshly baked cookies seemed to permeate the room. Prentiss suddenly realized she was starving.

Abner said, "You should try one. They're pretty damn good, if I do say so."

"No, thank you," Hotchner said, and gave their guest a smile. "We just got off break and we all had something then, but we appreciate the gift. Really, we do."

"You're welcome," Abner said. "Nothing's too good for you people. It's a thankless job, what you do, but we're damn glad you're here to do it."

Hotchner's smile was looking more and more strained. "Thank you again."

"Well, I guess I'll be going," Abner said, growing as uncomfortable as Hotchner. "I guess if you'd found the guy, we'd know about it, right? You haven't found him, have you?"

"We're working on it," Hotchner said.

"Good, good. Can't ask for more. Well, guess I'll be going."

And, with a little wave, he was gone.

"What was that?" Prentiss asked.

"I'm not quite sure," Hotchner said.

Reid reached toward the container.

Hotchner said, "I hope you're after a sample to take to the crime lab."

"Unfortunately, yes," Reid said. "You don't have to remind me that Daniel Abner hasn't been cleared as a suspect . . . and that some UnSubs like to inject themselves into the investigation."

Hotchner nodded. "He was one of the men who found the bodies of our *poisoning* victims; then he came in for questioning, now this. Yep—the cookies go to the lab first."

Taking the plastic container, Reid said glumly, "I'll do the deed."

He left the room with the cookies, staring at them in his grasp.

The aroma of the treats lingered, though, and Prentiss's stomach growled a little.

She considered going to the cop's break room for a snack (Hotch had been fibbing about them just having come off break). With any luck, there might be a banana or an apple in one of the vending machines. She had just pushed her chair back from the table when Garcia's face popped up on the screen.

Prentiss pulled the chair back in. "Do you have something?"

Garcia nodded excitedly. "We've identified one of the girls."

"Excellent."

Hotch leaned in.

Garcia was saying, "The most recent victim was a thirteen-year-old . . . well, she was thirteen at the time of her death, three when she disappeared. Her name was Heather Davison."

"Disappeared when she was *three*?" Prentiss asked, eyes wide. "Ten *years* ago?"

Garcia smirked humorlessly and nodded once. "Playing in her front yard. The phone rang in the house, her mother stepped inside for less than a minute, she said . . . and when Mommy came back out, little Heather was gone."

"Where did this happen?"

"Summerville, Georgia."

Prentiss frowned. "Where's that exactly?"

"Northwest of Atlanta, in the corner. Just east of Alabama and south of Chattanooga."

Prentiss was shaking her head. "The child was kidnapped ten years ago in Summerville, Georgia, and turns up dead and buried in Bemidji, Minnesota? How does that happen?"

With a wry little smile, Garcia said, "That I can't tell you. That's where you come in."

Prentiss sighed. "What else do you have on this?"

"Law enforcement did all they could. The AMBER Alert network wasn't in place yet, and no one would have thought of calling in the BAU back then, so they did things the old-fashioned way—followed a few clues until they petered out, and the case went cold. Heather's parents tried to keep it active, but there just weren't the resources that we have today. They did have DNA taken from themselves and a hairbrush that Heather had used. That was where the match came from."

Hotchner said, "Fine work, Garcia."

"Thank you, sir."

He turned to Prentiss. "All right, you look into the Davison girl and victimology. Reid, start trying to figure out what sort of occupation this UnSub has. We know he needs money, and if he's had at least one of these girls for ten years, he's probably not pumping gas somewhere."

Prentiss looked up to see another man standing in the doorway—small, wiry, in his early to mid-forties, dark hair parted, glasses thick within clear plastic frames.

"Excuse me," the man said.

"Yes?" Hotchner asked.

"My name is Lawrence Silvan. I work for Bassinko

Industries. The company asked me to stop by and offer our assistance."

"Come in, Mr. Silvan," Hotchner said, waving the man to an empty chair at the conference table.

Silvan nodded to Reid and Prentiss as he sat. He wore a gray suit with a white shirt and navy blue tie with gray stripes, not inexpensive attire but certifiably drab.

Hotchner asked, "Are you with the PR department, Mr. Silvan?"

The little man seemed surprised by that, then with a modest smile, said, "Oh no—I'm a forester."

"A lumberjack, you mean?" Prentiss asked. She would have made him for an accountant, given the man's stature and dress.

"No, no, a lumberjack *cuts down* trees—I *grow* them."

"A sylviculturist," Reid said.

"Yes—I got my degree from Iowa State in 1988. But most people just call us foresters."

Hotchner's face remained a blank mask, but his voice was somewhere between skeptical and curious. "If you're not in public relations, Mr. Silvan, may I ask why you're here?"

"As I said, to assist in your investigation, if you might find that helpful. Bassinko Industries is appalled that such a thing would happen on land we own. The company wants to do everything it can to assist in your catching this murderer."

Hotchner asked, "How do you think you can assist us?"

"The company thought you might have questions about the forest and forestry that I could answer. Things that would make your job easier in the long run."

"That could be very helpful," Hotchner said. "Thank you."

"There are three of us who inspect that particular forest from time to time, but it is predominantly my territory, which is why the company sent me to you." Silvan's eyes wandered around the room and the pictures and other posted materials on the walls. "It looks as though you have quite a bit going on already."

"Yes, we do," Hotchner said.

Reid said, "I do have a forestry question for you, sir."

Silvan turned toward him.

"We're operating on the grounds that this particular area means something to the UnSub. . . ." Reid explained the contraction, then went on. "As I said, we think the area may have some special meaning or connection to the UnSub. Can you think of anything that might fit into that theory?"

Silvan was shaking his head before Reid had finished speaking.

"Indian burial ground?" Reid asked. "Some sort of hallowed ground to the Native Americans?"

The forester could not contain his surprise. "You think someone from one of the reservations did this?"

"No, no," Reid said. "We're just trying to learn

why the UnSub chose this particular place to bury the victims."

Hotchner said sharply, "Mr. Silvan, we need anything you hear to stay in this room. Do you understand? This is an ongoing federal investigation."

Nodding vigorously, Silvan said, "I understand completely. I'm sorry to have jumped to a conclusion. It's just that I . . . I've never been around anything like this before."

Prentiss nodded her encouragement to him as the little man's eyes lighted on her for a second, then flew away.

Reid repeated, "Can you think of any reason for the UnSub to have chosen this place?"

Silvan considered the question. "Well, it's never been an Indian burial ground."

Reid's expression changed from quizzical to slightly disappointed.

"That area was harvested six years ago," Silvan said. "The site might have been chosen simply because your . . . UnSub . . . thought that very few folks would be in that forest for another forty years, at least."

Prentiss asked, "As the chief forester, aren't you in there regularly?"

Silvan nodded. "Either your UnSub didn't know that a forester regularly inspects the area, or he counted on us not checking that particular spot. There are nearly one hundred acres in that forest alone. It's a lot of ground to cover, and we don't study every single tree, every single time. Mostly, we monitor growth and make sure that insects, poisons, and even weeds are not interfering with the growth of the wood. In that way, forestry is little different than running a farm that grows corn or soybeans."

Hotchner glanced at the two agents. "Any other questions?"

Reid and Prentiss shook their heads.

Hotchner said, "Thank you for your time, Mr. Silvan. Do you have a card?"

The forester withdrew one from his jacket pocket. "The front has my contact information at the company, my cell number's on the back. Feel free to call any time."

"Thanks," Hotchner said. "We appreciate your company's help . . . and yours."

Rising, Silvan flashed a tiny, awkward smile, and said, "No problem, no problem at all."

When the man was gone, Hotchner turned to Prentiss, and went back to what they'd been discussing.

"We need to find out how long the UnSub keeps the girls," Hotch said. "The Davison girl disappeared ten years ago. How much of that time did she spend with the UnSub? The same is true of the others too. Did he only keep *one* for a long period, or all of them?"

Reid said, "That would seem inconvenient for a single man."

"That's right. And we know he's got to have a reasonably well-paying job, which means he probably isn't jumping job to job with great frequency. Does he work out of the house so he can keep the girls from escaping? Does he have a partner? Does he keep the girls at a remote location?"

Prentiss jotted notes as the boss spoke. Inside, her gut churned. They knew so little and had so many questions and at the same time, out there, somewhere, their UnSub might be getting ready to bury another teenage girl in the woods.

On his own, more leisurely but very deadly timetable.

Chapter Four

Bemidji, Minnesota

An hour or so after lunch, Rossi and Morgan finally returned with Detective Garue, who had a box of evidence in tow, which the local cop set down on the conference room table, and removed the lid.

Prentiss and Reid were still bent over the table, hard at it, Prentiss on her laptop, Reid poring over reports from the Davison kidnapping in Georgia. JJ was off dealing with both the media and the new tip hotline.

The group leader, Hotchner, was trying to figure out how best to utilize his people—he had an idea that might not go over well. But, then, that was the luxury of being the boss.

"Found the firearm," Rossi said matter-of-factly, holding up the bag that held the shotgun.

Brandishing a plastic evidence bag, Garue said, "And we also came up with about half an ounce of weed"—he nodded toward the box—"not to mention a championship smut collection."

"What we didn't find," Morgan said rather glumly,

"was any sign that those girls—or *any* children, for that matter—ever set foot in Rohl's house."

"Nothing at all?" Prentiss asked.

Finding a seat at the table, Rossi shook his head. "If this is our guy, he's been holding the girls somewhere else. And that was definitely not a dwelling where some mastermind had surgically removed the evidence."

"If he's our bad guy, he's good," Morgan said, also taking a seat (as had Garue). "Didn't even find so much as a key that didn't fit some lock or other we ran across."

Rossi picked up: "If he had the girls somewhere else, either they weren't under lock and key or he has that key hidden somewhere else, too . . . because it is sure as hell *not* in that house. Which, by the way, is a dump."

Prentiss smirked. "We gathered."

Hotchner asked, "So—do you still think he's the UnSub?"

"Not out of the question," Rossi said, with an eyebrow shrug. "We definitely have more digging to do."

Hotchner gestured toward the nearest laptop. "I'll get Garcia to contact Arkansas and see what else we can learn on that end."

Garue said, "With the weapons and drugs charges? He's not going anywhere for a while."

Morgan lifted a forefinger. "Don't forget he assaulted a federal officer."

Garue nodded. "He's definitely going to be a guest of the county for a while."

Rossi asked, "Anything go down here at the fort while we were out doing God's work?"

Hotchner filled them in on the visits by Abner and Lawrence Silvan.

Rossi's eyebrows were up and he seemed vaguely amused. "Cookies, Aaron? And of course you sent them to the crime lab."

Hotchner said nothing.

Rossi told his old friend, "Generous of you. You *do* know we haven't eaten since breakfast?"

With no apparent recognition that he was being kidded, Hotchner said, "There's food in the vending machine in the break room."

Rossi chuckled and shook his head. Garue was looking at Morgan, with an expression that asked, *Is your boss for real?* But Morgan offered no help.

Hotchner filled them in on the identity of the Davison girl and what they knew about that case, so far.

Rossi, dead serious now, said, "Georgia's a long way from Minnesota."

"It's a long way coming *or* going," Morgan said. "Was the Davison girl registered in school anywhere around here?"

Hotchner shook his head. "Not that we know, but it's early on that score. We haven't had time to put together a digital aging photo."

Such a photo would show what the victim might look like today.

"And," Hotchner continued, "we'll get a forensics

sculptor to do a 3-D representation, but the truth is, that's going to take a while."

"So," Rossi said, "what's next?"

Before Hotchner could answer, JJ came into the room in a rush.

"Victim number two has been identified," she said. "Lee Ann Clark, kidnapped from a park near her family's residence in Heflin, Alabama."

"When?" Hotchner asked.

"Ten years ago," JJ said, "within just two weeks of Heather Davison."

"Nice work. How did you manage it?"

"Credit Garcia—she just got notified there was another DNA hit."

Hotchner swung his attention toward Reid. "Let's get Garcia on the linkup and find out more."

In a few seconds, Reid had made that happen.

"Garcia," Hotchner said.

"Sir?"

"What have you found out about our second victim?"

"She was three and a half at the time of her abduction—which was less than two weeks after the kidnapping of Heather Davison. Lee Ann Clark was playing in a park not even three blocks from her house when the abduction went down."

"Certainly a child that age hadn't been left alone . . . ?"

"No, both her parents and a slightly older brother were there. They were distracted for just a moment and when they turned back, Lee Ann was gone."

Hotchner frowned. "Distracted by what?"

"The brother, five at the time, was on the monkey bars. He slipped and both Mom and Dad turned when they heard him yell in pain. That was all it took."

Reid asked, "And no one else on the scene saw anything?"

"No."

Hotchner said, "No surprise. People in a park tend to be focused on their own activities. . . . Keep digging."

"Will do."

"And, Garcia—see what progress has been made on the third victim. Plus, start running down missing blonde girls from the South who disappeared around ten years ago."

"Yes, sir."

"And expand your search to the corridor between Bemidji and Atlanta."

"Right," Garcia said, then disappeared to do her work.

Rossi asked, "You're thinking the UnSub may have lived in the Atlanta area?"

Hotchner said, "I'm thinking it's a place to start. Both girls disappeared from a hundred-square-mile area, so I'm guessing our UnSub spent some time there. There's one sure way to find out."

Rossi, ahead of him, said, "You really want to split the team up like that?"

Hotchner said, "You'll be as close as the nearest phone or laptop."

Frowning, Prentiss asked, "What I am missing?"

Hotchner said to her, "You and Rossi take the jet to the Atlanta field office and see what you can find out at that end. The rest of us will work the case from here."

Prentiss said to Rossi, "How did you know us going to Atlanta was what Hotch was thinking?"

Deadpan, Rossi said to her, "Haven't you heard? I'm a profiler."

Atlanta, Georgia

David Rossi was well and truly used to not waking up in his own bed.

Life on the road was part of not only his BAU job, but his role as writer and lecturer, which kept him frequently away from home as well. Waking up in his second city on one case, however, was not the norm. Still, he wouldn't miss the Arctic Circle temperatures of Minnesota, and had no problem with waking in the more temperate climes of Atlanta.

The flight into Hartsfield International Airport had been both uneventful and late. He and Prentiss had not left until the afternoon, which meant the pair didn't land at Hartsfield until nearly ten p.m. local time. Having skipped lunch and losing an hour entering the eastern time zone, Rossi was starving by the time they landed.

He and Prentiss had shared a late dinner in the hotel restaurant, a typically mediocre dining experience, and he relished every forkful. Scotty Carlyle, the rangy African-American agent who'd picked them up at the airport, kept them company, not joining them, just sipping on a Diet Coke.

Built like a linebacker, Carlyle had close-clipped hair, wide, clear brown eyes, and a mellow baritone touched with a Southern accent.

Carlyle asked, "What brings you to Atlanta to investigate a ten-year-old kidnapping?"

Rossi and Prentiss brought the agent up to speed on their case.

"Hell of a thing," Carlyle said. "You think you have a serial killer, operating undetected over a long period like this? Is that unusual?"

"I wish it were," Rossi said. "This is probably the worst kind of serial killer to identify and track—on the move, striking periodically."

"Even in these days of computers and DNA?"

"Less tough, sure, but yeah. Even the most sophisticated computer systems provide cracks a killer like this can fall through."

Carlyle shook his head, sipped his Diet Coke. "So . . . what do you have in mind for tomorrow?"

Rossi told him.

Now, having slept, showered and shaved—and after a light breakfast with Prentiss—Rossi felt ready to face the day and find out what connected Bemidji, Minnesota, to Summerville, Georgia, and Heflin, Alabama.

Prentiss—in gray slacks, a navy blue blouse, and dark shoes, her weapon on her hip under a gray jacket—stepped out into the sunshine at the hotel's entrance. Rossi—as usual in jeans, with a blue work shirt and a red tie full of geometric shapes under a navy sport coat, his gun on his right hip—enjoyed the warmth, lifting his face toward the sky.

Prentiss smiled at him. "Not so terrible, trading this in for Minnesota."

"Doesn't suck," he admitted.

Carlyle pulled up in a black Tahoe. When they commented on the lovely day, he didn't seem to know what they were talking about, clearly not nearly as impressed with the local weather as the visitors were.

With Rossi in the front seat and Prentiss in back, Carlyle drove them north on I-75, getting off at the Adairsville exit. From there it was two-lane roads, state 140 and U.S. 27 through the edge of the Chattahoochee National Forest and onto the east side of Summerville in Chattooga County, only a few miles from the Alabama border.

A sleepy little berg, home to around five thousand, Summerville had no police department and a handful of stoplights. The sheriff's office—a small one-story building—was just off Commerce Street, the main drag, at 35 W Washington.

The front door was off to the right, the remainder of the building's facade a huge picture window. As with many small-town departments, this was not the most secure building in the world. They entered, Rossi in the lead, followed by Prentiss and Carlyle.

The waist-high wall ran the width of the lobby, a single deputy behind it on a chair-back stool. The broad-shouldered young deputy—with the kind of crew cut you saw mostly on military bases—greeted them with a professional smile. "May I help you?"

Rossi flashed his credentials, introduced himself and the others, as the deputy got to his feet and regarded them, agape.

"Truth is," the deputy said with a Barney Fife–worthy grin, "I never met an FBI agent before."

"And now you have," Rossi said pleasantly. "Is the sheriff in?"

"Sheriff Burke?"

Rossi felt he was showing considerable restraint by not asking if this county had more than one sheriff. "Yes, thanks. Sheriff Burke will be fine."

The deputy signaled for them to pass through the gate and they did, and led them to a glass-enclosed office in the left-rear corner behind the bull pen area. He knocked and the sheriff—at his desk, on the phone—glanced up and waved him inside.

Rossi took the liberty of following the deputy in, and so did Prentiss and Carlyle.

The sheriff said, "There's some folks here, Sam— I'll talk at ya later."

He cradled the phone and rose, a man about Rossi's height and weight, and maybe five years younger. His hair was a short mop of curly brown and he was summer-tanned in November.

The deputy said, "These folks are from the FBI."

Unhesitatingly sticking out his hand, the sheriff said, "Ted Burke."

"Supervisory Special Agent David Rossi." The profiler displayed his credentials with one hand and shook hands using the other, then introduced Prentiss and Carlyle, who also shook hands with the friendly, no-nonsense sheriff.

"Bring us in another chair, will you, son?"

"Yes, sir," the deputy said, and went out.

The office wasn't spacious but they weren't particularly crowded, three visitors and the sheriff. A big blond desk dominated with an oxblood-colored leather chair behind it. File cabinets lined a side wall, and a table stacked with circulars and other paper was opposite. Behind the sheriff was a window with drawn blinds and, all around it, framed diplomas and citations.

Rossi and Prentiss took the two visitor chairs and then the deputy was back with another chair for Carlyle.

Rossi said, "We understand we're going back a few years. But we'd like to talk to you about the Heather Davison disappearance."

Burke's friendly expression darkened. "What a terrible, sad deal that was."

"You were sheriff then?"

"No," Burke said, "but I was here, all right—a deputy back then."

"Did you work the case?"

"I did. I was lead investigator, in fact."

That was a nice break, Rossi thought.

"We haven't told the parents yet," Rossi said, sitting forward. "But we've identified Heather Davison's remains from a grave near Bemidji, Minnesota."

Burke closed his eyes. Several seconds passed; then the sheriff said, "I was afraid of that when I was asked to pass along those DNA samples. Been waitin' for the shoe to drop, ever since."

Rossi asked, "Do her parents still live locally?"

"Yeah—Davison family's been here since the place was called Selma, back in the 1830s."

"Before we inform them," Rossi said, "we'd appreciate it if you'd tell us about the case."

The sheriff's smile was melancholy. "No fun, bein' the messenger of such news, huh? You folks wouldn't be stallin', would you?"

"Well, this is information we need," Rossi said. "But you may be right—I've had to tell too many parents that their child is never coming home."

"I hear that," he said, and sighed. "Davisons are good people. I've known their families since we were all just little kids. Jim manages a warehouse down in Rome, and Kelly is a stay-at-home mom . . . least she was back then. Those two doted on that little girl. They had a lot of trouble havin' a child."

Rossi cocked his head. "You were close enough to know something that intimate?"

"Hell, Agent Rossi—it's a small town and everybody knows everybody else's business."

"I understand," Rossi said, but he didn't really, never having lived in a hamlet like this one.

"Anyway," the sheriff was saying, "everybody thought it was a blessing when little Heather showed up, after Jim and Kelly tried so hard for so long. Then to have *this* tragedy happen . . ."

"What can you tell us about the investigation?"

Sheriff Burke leaned back in his chair and mulled that for a while. Rossi could tell the man had his own pace, and prodding him would be useless.

Finally the sheriff said, "As investigations go, it was by-the-numbers, every step of the way. We even had some of your FBI boys down here, helping out. . . ."

The sheriff's accent made that sound like "hepping."

"But it was like that little girl, she just wandered to the edge of the planet and fell off. If you'd come here today to tell me you had proof she'd been abducted by aliens, I don't know that I wouldn't have believed you."

"No physical evidence?"

"All we had was one small piece of a taillight on a muddy shoulder in front of the house—that was all she wrote. Bastard—pardon my French, ma'am— must've backed into the tree near the street. Nobody saw a damned thing that day, though."

Prentiss asked, "No one saw anything suspicious at all?"

Burke shook his head. "One minute that precious child was in the yard, next she was gone. My gut always told me it was someone from out of town, some predator just swung through trollin' . . . but, like I say, there were no clues, beyond that piece of taillight, the size of a quarter."

Prentiss asked, "What makes you think it was someone from out of town?"

"Again, you know everybody in a town this size. That means you also know the ones that are goddamn child molesters, too. . . . Again, pardon my French. . . ."

"It's okay," Prentiss said with a smile. "I speak the language."

The sheriff liked that and smiled back at her; but then he grew serious again as he said, "There's a couple of those types in town, and I knew them as well then as I do now. If they'da done it . . . well, let's just say we'd have found out."

Rossi watched as Prentiss's face went from perplexed to disapproving. He shot her a look and she wiped her expression clean.

But Burke had caught it. "You have to understand, ma'am, down here? There's legal, and then there's justice—especially when it comes to crimes against children."

"I understand," Prentiss said.

Rossi nodded at her and gave her a small smile—she didn't have to condone the sheriff's point of view to fathom it. And this man seemed helpful, so slack would be cut. . . .

"That little girl coulda become any darn thing when she grew up," Burke said, and his voice caught for a moment. "Pretty little thing might've been Miss Georgia, and she was a smart little thing, too—maybe she woulda been the doctor cured cancer, or president someday, only this evil son of a bitch took any kind of possibility away from her."

Carefully, Rossi said, "You took this personally."

"Hell, man, we all did. Town like this, she's not just another little girl. I don't mean to suggest she's just a statistic to you people. I know you do good work and you try to help out, but when you've investigated a hundred kidnappings, the kids tend to blur together—that's understandable; that's human nature. Here, though, something like a little girl getting kidnapped just doesn't happen, only when it does, that one girl becomes a very big damn deal. So, no offense, but other than being the ones to tell those nice people they're never going to see their daughter again? I'm not sure how much you can help."

"I understand where you're coming from, Sheriff," Rossi said. "But we're part of a small unit of investigators who make a point of getting to know the victims. They are in no way statistics to us."

"I said I meant no offense. It's just, this has to be one damn cold case at this point. . . ."

"It's warming up, sir, or we wouldn't be here."

"Well, that is a point, isn't it?"

"Yes, it is. And here's another point—something that goes along with investigating hundreds of kidnappings—we are also really, really good at this."

Burke nodded, but whether he was convinced remained a mystery.

"We'll help you here," Rossi said. "There wasn't much to go on back then, but we've got more now."

"I'll take any help I can get," Burke said, "but after all this time, I just don't know what there is to do."

Prentiss leaned forward. "Let's start with your notion that the perpetrator had to be someone from outside Summerville. That has to come from more than just you knowing who the local sex offenders are."

The sheriff shifted in his chair. "Well, no one in the neighborhood saw out-of-state plates around the time Heather was abducted. Around here, out-of-state plates stick out like sore thumbs. If somebody saw a car they didn't recognize, or was from somewhere's else? They woulda said something, after Heather went missing."

Rossi nodded and asked, "What about out-of-*county* plates?"

"That mighta slipped by, especially if it was a county on the plate that looks similar to Chatooga—Chattahoochee and Catoosa counties don't look all that much different, if you only catch 'em for a second, or from a distance. Chattahoochee is down south by Columbus."

Rossi looked at Carlyle.

"Southwest of Atlanta," the big agent said.

Burke said, "On the other hand, Catoosa County is right up by Chattanooga. That's not far away at all."

These nonsense names were starting to sound like a Dr. Seuss story to Rossi.

"This car would be nondescript," Rossi said. "The Unknown Subject has successfully abducted at least three girls, and left nothing substantial behind but one busted taillight."

"That taillight, though—it's not from a car."

"Really?" Rossi asked. "You sent the piece of tail-light to the FBI lab?"

"Sure we did, and what we got back was it belonged to a 1993 Ford Aerostar."

"Your basic soccer-mom van."

Burke nodded. "Hell, even then they were everywhere."

Rossi said, "Nondescript enough to blend in."

"Wish I had something for you more distinctive," Burke said. "But the bad guys aren't that cooperative around here."

Prentiss smiled. "Not around anywhere."

Rossi said, "You knew there was another abduction not far away from here."

It was not a question.

The sheriff nodded. "Lee Ann Clark, over in Heflin, Alabama. We swapped information . . . but hell, they had even less to go on than we did."

"Did you consider going in together? On a task force?"

Burke's eyes went wide and he smiled. "Uh . . . do we look like a task-force-type operation, Agent Rossi?"

"Sorry," Rossi said, smiling back. "Anyway, we'll be digging deeper now. We'll find this Unknown Subject—trust us. This is what we do, and we do it well."

"I like your confidence," Burke said.

"Thanks."

"Of course, some confident people are full of crap."

"True. Now . . . you want to show us where the Davisons live? We have some bad news to deliver. . . ."

Ten minutes later, Carlyle was pulling up in front of a well-kept bungalow in a quiet residential neighborhood only blocks from the sheriff's office. Light blue with pale yellow shutters, the house stood out among the many white houses lining the street. The elm tree that had provided the only clue in the girl's kidnapping was considerably taller now and provided shade.

Automatically, Rossi profiled the neighborhood. Almost noon on a sunny November weekday, and the street was Sunday quiet—not so much as a dog barking. Very few cars parked in front of homes or in driveways—this lower-middle-class neighborhood would be made up mostly of families where both spouses worked. Children would be in school and the rest either in preschool or day care. Avoiding the fifteen minutes the postman was on the block, the UnSub had a better than fifty-fifty chance that not a single person would have thought anything of a minivan with Georgia plates.

Rossi turned toward the Davison house and tried to see what the kidnapper saw. Had this house been stalked, staked out, cased? Or had this been a snatch-and-grab job, a crime of opportunity? Right now he didn't have enough information. And he knew what they had to do next.

He hated this part of the job. There was never an easy way to break this kind of loss to a family. A spouse or sibling, or even a parent, that was one thing, but to tell a mother and/or a father they would never see their child again, that was the worst of the worst, not only wounding the recipients, but the messenger as well—and Rossi already had his share of scars.

Burke led them up to the door, and Rossi knocked. They only had to wait for a moment before the door opened and a woman in her early thirties filled the frame.

She had short curly brown hair and wide blue eyes behind large, circular wire-frame glasses. Petite, she wore jeans and a red University of Georgia T-shirt.

"Why, Sheriff Burke," she said, voice trembling.

"Hi, Kelly—these folks are from the Behavioral Analysis Unit of the FBI. They'd like to talk to you. Might we come in?"

Her face turned white as a blister. Then she stepped aside, letting them into a small living room. An entertainment center was along a wall, but the DVD player or the big-screen TV wasn't what caught Rossi's interest. One shelf of the big, Mission-style cabinet was given over to pictures of Heather Davison—an altar of framed photos charting her life from adorable infant to the bubbly three-year-old she'd been when she disappeared.

A floral sofa took one wall; a beige recliner was at an angle by the picture window. Another wall was home to a table, a wing chair and framed photos, friends and relatives, but Heather wasn't in any of these shots.

The agents and the sheriff remained standing, getting out of Mrs. Davison's way as she went to the sofa. "Won't you all sit down, please?"

Prentiss took the wing chair, Sheriff Burke perched on the recliner, and Carlyle stood near the door. Rossi sat beside Mrs. Davison on the sofa, but gave her plenty of room.

"Jim won't be home from work," she said, "for several hours. . . ."

Burke nodded, his expression somber. "I've sent two fellas over to Rome to make sure he gets home all right."

"This isn't good news, is it? You didn't send deputies for him so he could be here when you bring Heather home . . . did you?"

Rossi leaned forward. "Mrs. Davison, my name is David Rossi, this is Agent Emily Prentiss and that's Agent Scotty Carlyle."

Mrs. Davison nodded numbly, a tear trickling. Prentiss got a tissue from her purse for the woman.

Rossi said, "You provided a DNA sample. So did your husband, and we had hair from your daughter's brush."

Rocking gently now as she wept, Mrs. Davison bit her lower lip.

Stomach churning, Rossi wanted to rise and flee from this house and never look back. Not an option. Not an option. Nor could he just stop and remain silent and let the woman cry herself out. She knew, she already knew, everyone in this room knew. So did the neighbors, seeing the police car out front, and in a town this size, by the end of lunch hour every citizen would know.

Yet Rossi still had to say it. The loss would not be completely real to this woman until spoken out loud.

"Three hunters found Heather buried in a grave in the woods near Bemidji, Minnesota, last Saturday. Yesterday we were able to confirm her identity."

The wail that came out of the woman was like an animal dying. Rossi sat mute, something dying in him, too, in a much smaller way, but dying. Finally, the profiler managed to touch her hand, finding it cold, as if all the blood had drained out. Ineffectually, he patted her shoulder as she covered her face with her hands and wept as though she would never stop.

They sat that way for nearly half an hour, three silent strangers and an equally silent acquaintance trying to console a woman who had lost the most important part of herself ten years ago and now, after a decade of aching, of having to bear that emptiness echoing through every nanosecond, she had just been informed that her loss was permanent, her grief terminal.

After thirty-some minutes that seemed forever to Rossi, the deputies arrived home with Mr. Davison. Normally, he would have seemed a good-looking young man—close-cropped brown hair, wide-set, earnest brown eyes; in a well-tailored brown suit with a tan shirt and a brown-and-tan-striped tie.

Right now, at this terrible moment, his face was red and his eyes bloodshot, a deputy staying close to him as the husband crossed to his wife. Rossi rose and made room so the grieving parents could share the sofa.

At least now the Davisons knew the truth.

Rossi would want to interview them again, but not today. Their grief was too raw, their pain too deep.

For that, Rossi had no solution. All he could do now was catch the UnSub who had maimed this family, and stop him from doing this again.

Bemidji, Minnesota

He adored His Beloved.

Worshipped the ground she walked on. The cliché was not the least bit bothersome to him. Of course, she wasn't perfect, he knew that, but that just made her that much more attractive to him. She was, he knew, the best thing that had ever happened to him. When she was happy, she was the greatest gift a man could have.

But when she was in the throes of melancholia, as she was now, it sapped his very soul and made him every bit as sad as she. He had a head start this time. He had loved Paula, the name they'd given the blonde girl when she came into their lives ten years ago. Paula being sent to "finishing school," as they called it, had been a crushing blow for him.

He had tried to talk His Beloved out of doing this again. "I love Paula—can't we *keep* her?"

She had shaken her head. "We have to protect

her. Now that she's ready for finishing school, there's nothing else that can be done."

"But I love the child, don't you?"

"You *know* I do," she said. "I love her so much that I can't let her stay. One of us has to be strong. Do I have to remind you what happened when my father told me he loved me?"

There was no talking to her after that.

Now, sitting at the dinner table—with her across from him more morose than ever, picking at her food, not really eating—he decided it was time.

Knowing better, he asked, "Are you all right, dear?"

She didn't answer for a while, her fork making lazy circles in her mashed potatoes as she considered the question. Just when he was beginning to think she hadn't heard him, she said, "You know, the house sounds so empty now, without the happy sound of our girls."

"Oh, I know," he said quietly. He wanted to say that right now things would be better, if Paula had not been sent to finishing school, but what good would it do? What was done was done. Instead, he chose to bring her some joy.

"It's funny you mention that," he said. "I've been doing a little shopping."

Her face brightened slightly. "You don't think it's too soon?"

Smiling at her, he said, "Not if it will make you happy, dear."

She beamed at him. "It would make me *so* happy if we could be a family again."

He nodded. "Then, that's what we'll do. We'll start a new family. I know right where to begin."

She touched his hand across the table. "I love you."

The emotion swept through him.

He adored His Beloved.

Chapter Five

Bemidji, Minnesota

With Prentiss and Rossi in Georgia, the rest of the BAU team was working longer hours, the leads growing colder as their patience wore thin even as they dug deeper and deeper, always coming up empty.

Although they still had Billy Rohl (aka Kwitcher) in custody for violating his sexual predator status in Arkansas and Minnesota (as well as his pot stash, plus assault on Prentiss), no evidence had been turned up tying the sex offender to the murders of the three girls—other than Billy being the one who'd found the bodies. Or anyway, the first body.

As far as Derek Morgan was concerned, the only good news in the last twenty-four hours was that the cookies brought in by Daniel Abner had proved to be both unpoisoned and delicious. The downside was the local crime lab techs had gobbled up most of them, perhaps to fully confirm the cookies were truly safe.

Still, the rotund hunting guide who'd generously contributed the sweets remained a suspect, if not a good one in Detective Garue's opinion; but Hotchner had Reid checking into the man's background, anyway.

Most disturbing—and promising—was the status of the third member of the hunting party, Logan Tweed, who had dropped out of sight. They'd been to his home, but no one answered the door. They'd phoned his house and received no answer—ditto with his cell phone—and someone at the construction company where Tweed worked informed Morgan that "Lowg" was off on vacation, and they had no idea where he was. So far, at least, Tweed was just another dead end.

This afternoon, Morgan was charged with interviewing Rohl. Though their suspect would've been only around twenty when the girls disappeared, Rohl had lived seven and a half hours from Heflin, Alabama, and less than eight and a half hours from Summerville, Georgia. Not exactly right across the street, but hardly an insurmountable distance—not more than a day's drive for a dedicated sexual predator.

Plus, after exploring the evidence from Rohl's house—and after a quick update from Garcia concerning the taillight evidence in Georgia—Morgan had some new questions for the child molester.

Rohl was already in the visitors' room of the Beltrami County Jail. Wearing an orange jumpsuit, his hands cuffed through a ring welded to the metal table, Rohl looked like hell, his beard a scraggly mess. And he had the red-rimmed eyes of someone who had not slept very well on his first night in jail.

The prisoner looked up at Morgan and rolled his eyes. "Not *you* again. . . ."

Morgan flashed his killer grin. "Billy, I'm hurt—aren't you happy to see me?" The profiler took the seat across from his suspect, setting a manila folder on the table between them.

Rohl nodded toward the empty chair next to him. "Does my lawyer know you're here?"

"Sure he does," Morgan said. "The thing about public defenders is, they're busy. Still, you'd think he'd be here, since I told him what time we were meeting. And I'm pretty sure he knows how serious this all is."

Rohl frowned. His reply was as pouty as a child's, ironic considering his favorite pastime. "You can't talk to me without my lawyer present."

"I can, if you're in the mood to talk."

"Well, I'm not!"

Morgan grinned and shrugged, his voice pleasant as he said, "Well, then, we'll wait. I don't know about you, Billy, but I have nothing else planned."

Rohl rolled his eyes.

As the two men sat mutely across from each other, Morgan nonchalantly tapped the manila folder, fingers gently drumming. Rohl glanced up now and then, but mostly stared at the cuffs at his wrists.

Morgan had no intention of violating Rohl's civil rights—that simply wasn't the way the agent operated. But, if he sat here long enough without saying anything, he had a hunch Rohl would be unable to resist blabbing. And, as a profiler, Morgan found his hunches often panned out.

And after ten minutes, sure enough, Rohl cleared his throat and was obviously just about to speak when the door behind Morgan opened and someone came in.

The agent didn't even have to turn around. The relief on Rohl's face told Morgan that Tim Staten, the suspect's attorney, had entered.

Anger edging his voice, Staten demanded, "What the hell is this?"

"You knew when the meeting was scheduled, counselor," Morgan said. "Just waiting for you."

Staten went around the table to stand beside his client, and glared down at Morgan. Despite his lack of height and soft-around-the-waist build, Staten was an imposing man; bald, and with metal-frame glasses that intensified the glare of steel gray eyes, he reminded Morgan of a human pit bull. Staten's brown double-breasted suit, white shirt and brown tie with tan stripes said *money* to the profiler, who guessed the court-appointed attorney must have been doing pro bono work in addition to a prosperous practice.

Turning to Rohl, Staten said, "Did he ask you any questions?"

Rohl thought about that.

"I asked Billy if he was happy to see me," Morgan said. "He didn't answer—I think he realized it was a rhetorical question."

"He didn't answer," Staten said flatly, "because he has nothing to say to you." He gave his client a fatherly smile. "It's nice to have a client who actually listens to his attorney."

"I'm sure it is," Morgan said.

"Then why are we here? There's already been an interview *without* Mr. Rohl's counsel present."

"Which we stopped when he requested representation."

"Very generous of you. Again—why are we *here*, Agent Morgan?"

"I've got a few new questions."

Staten took the seat next to his client, glancing from Rohl to Morgan. "Such as?"

Morgan addressed the suspect. "When you lived in Arkansas, Billy, did you ever take trips?"

Rohl looked to his attorney, who nodded.

"Everybody takes trips," Rohl said.

"Ever been to Georgia?"

The suspect shook his head.

"You're sure? Little town named Summerville?" Morgan watched for any sign from Rohl that the name of the town had resonance.

Rohl said, "Never even heard of it."

"What about Heflin?"

"Georgia?"

"Alabama."

". . . No." Rohl's brow knit in thought. "I was in *Mississippi* once, though."

This felt like the truth to Morgan, who didn't think Rohl likely to be that good an actor—the man didn't seem bright enough. "Let's stick with Arkansas, Billy."

Staten and Rohl both sat silently.

"Let's take it back to 1998," Morgan said. "Do you remember what kind of car you drove?"

Rohl frowned in confusion. Staten appeared skeptical, but did not interrupt.

"Say what?" the suspect asked.

Morgan repeated the question.

"I had an 'eighty-six Cavalier," Rohl said before his lawyer could stop him. "That's a Chevy."

"Just the one vehicle?" Morgan asked.

"Just the one." The subject of automobiles seemed to lubricate Rohl's memory and his mouth. "That Cavalier was a piece of shit, but I had it from when I was in high school until 2005. Didn't get much use when I was locked up, so I just hung on to the puppy. Mileage was pretty low. Anyway, once I got a job and got some money, I picked up a cherry used 'oh two Grand Am. I still got that—why?"

"He's trying," Staten said to his client, with strained patience, "to ascertain if you kidnapped those children."

"Your counsel's right," Morgan admitted. "But that's not the only reason I ask."

Rohl looked at his lawyer, who was studying Morgan suspiciously.

Withdrawing a series of photos from the folder, Morgan said, "We found your secret smut collection in its hidey-hole in your bedroom closet."

Rohl paled and Staten's expression turned stricken.

"Nude pictures of girls from the Internet, magazines, and videos—most of the girls appear to be underage."

Staten started to protest, but Morgan cut him off.

"You'll want to know about this, counselor." To Rohl, he said, "From our perspective, the most interesting find was the photos you apparently took yourself, Billy—of teenage girls in front of the Bemidji Middle School and High School. Harmless amateur photography, in and of themselves, until we remember that you, Billy, are a sex offender."

Rohl bowed his head in silence—in what might have been prayer. If Rohl was praying, Morgan hoped the creep got a busy signal.

Staten began a blustering response, but Morgan paid him scant attention. What they had of the profile, so far, fit Rohl in several respects. Billy was still their best suspect; but Morgan would have been happier had Rohl admitted to at some point owning a van.

Morgan, his voice not unfriendly, asked, "You want to tell me something, Billy, and do yourself some good?"

Staten frowned, but Rohl nodded rapidly.

The attorney asked, "What kind of help would that be, Agent Morgan . . . and what's it worth to my client?"

"It's worth a word to the judge that he cooperated . . . but I'll need concrete information."

Staten shrugged. "Well, that's weak. He helps you out, he walks." The attorney seemed to once again feel on firmer ground.

Morgan replaced the photos in the folder, and rose. "No way he walks, counselor. Besides, what I wanted isn't really worth even a word to the judge. I was just trying to be helpful."

Morgan was about to knock to get the guard's attention when Staten said, "A word to the judge *could* be helpful, Agent Morgan. Let's hear what you want."

Slowly, the profiler turned. "I have only one question. Where is Logan Tweed?"

Rohl frowned and shrugged. "How the hell would *I* know?"

Staten didn't miss a beat. "I expect you to be as good as your word. My client has been entirely forthcoming."

"If he has been truthful about Tweed," Morgan said, "I'll stick to what I said. But if we turn Tweed up, and find out Billy knew where the man was but lied about it? . . . Well, draw your own conclusion, counselor."

Then Morgan knocked for the guard, who, in a few seconds, came and let him out.

Ten minutes later, having stopped for a cup of coffee on the way back, Morgan entered the conference room to find JJ, Reid, and Hotchner working on different aspects of the case. The pieces of the profile were coming together, but since going over the crime scenes, they had learned little. He hoped Rossi and Prentiss were having better luck in Georgia.

Morgan asked, "Did I miss anything?"

Hotchner shook his head.

Reid lifted his eyebrows and said, "Victimology would be a lot easier, if we actually knew something about these girls. Problem is, they were kidnapped nearly a decade ago, but was their abductor the same person who killed them? And if so, why does he keep them ten years, and then kill them?"

No one had an answer for that.

"The hotline is being flooded," JJ said, and her eyes widened in "here we go again" fashion. "The media will break the names of the two identified victims by tonight. The hotline will *really* be inundated, once people find out how far away from here the victims originally lived . . . and how much time has passed since their disappearance."

Morgan was just about to take a seat facing the door when he saw Daniel Abner getting ready to knock on the frame.

"Mr. Abner," Morgan said. "May I help you?"

The human fireplug wore his usual flannel shirt and jeans with brown work boots. He'd been intent enough on knocking that he stopped just short of the frame and jumped a little when Morgan spoke.

Abner said, "I just wanted to stop and see how you folks are getting along."

Hotchner, just short of cold, said from his seat at the table, "We're still working hard on the case."

Entering, Abner asked, "Did you like the cookies?"

JJ rose and intercepted the hunting guide before he got too deep into the room.

"They were delicious," she said. "We shared them with others around here, and everyone wants to thank you again for them."

She had a hand on his shoulder now, trying to herd him back out. He managed to put on the brakes. Morgan started around the table, just in case, and Abner turned and faced him, the man's face as gray as concrete, but his eyes burning.

"Word is," he said, "you got Billy Kwitcher locked up for this—is that true?"

Morgan said, "An unrelated charge. He assaulted a federal officer."

Trembling with barely controlled rage, Abner said, "You need him to talk, you give *me* five minutes with the boy. Nobody ever need know."

Hotchner rose and came around. His voice hard now, the BAU leader said, "Mr. Abner, we have this under control. If you don't mind, my people and I need to get back to work."

With a quick nod, Abner said, "I understand. I'm just saying, if you need anything, don't hesitate to call."

The ice in his voice apparent now, Hotchner said, "*Thank* you."

Having a thought, Morgan said, "Just one moment, before you go, Mr. Abner—would you happen to have any idea where Logan Tweed is?"

"Well . . . over at that construction outfit, I suppose. Why?"

Morgan shook his head, and gave the time-honored *Dragnet* response: "Just a routine part of the investigation."

Hotchner said, "JJ—a word?"

She came over.

Whispering, her boss said, "Tell these locals to at least warn us when he's in the building."

She nodded.

Abner was frowning when JJ took him by the arm and walked him out, making innocuous conversation.

When the pair was down the hall, out of earshot, Hotchner turned to Reid. "Get Garcia. I want to know everything about our helpful Mr. Abner before the end of business today."

Reid said he'd get right on it, and—in less than a minute—they were gathered around Reid's laptop, Garcia smiling at them. "So, how are things in Twin Peaks?"

That got several smiles from the profilers, with the exception of Hotchner, who either didn't understand the pop culture reference or didn't care, and just crisply explained what information he wanted about Daniel Abner.

"I'll get on that," she said, and her usual cheery smile disappeared and her demeanor darkened, "but first I should pass along some information I just received from the lab. They've identified the third victim—Abigail Mathis. She was kidnapped from her home in Jesup, Georgia, as her parents slept in the next room."

Hotchner asked, "When was the crime?"

Garcia's eyes darted to another screen; then she was facing them again. "June of 1998—less than a week before Heather Davison was abducted across the state in Summerville."

Morgan frowned. *Why were these kidnappings clustered like this?*

Hotchner asked, "How old was the Mathis girl?"

"Time of the abduction, not quite four."

The faces surrounding the laptop were grave.

Hotchner asked, "Any clues?"

Garcia shook her head. "Not much. A man's size-ten work boot in the backyard, under the girl's bedroom window. The ground was soft because it rained the day before. The screen was cut, the window open, because it was a warm night. Then the little girl was gone."

Hotchner asked, "Anything on the boot?"

"A Wolverine, very popular. Popular size, as well. Both the locals and the bureau tried to run it down, but got nowhere with it."

"Thanks, Garcia," Hotchner said. "We appreciate the good, hard work. Don't be shy about sending us updates."

"I won't be, sir," she said, then clicked off.

Turning to Morgan and Reid, Hotchner said, "Both the other crimes seem more spontaneous—smash and grab—but this one, he had to plan a little at least."

Morgan said, "Plus, he broke into an occupied home and stole a child without alarming anyone else in the house."

Hotchner nodded somberly. "Our UnSub has skills we were unaware of. Let's incorporate this information into the profile. Also, let's get on the phone to Rossi and Prentiss, and get them up to speed."

Heflin, Alabama

The black SUV bearing SSA's Rossi and Prentiss, with SA Carlyle at the wheel, made its way west, chasing the afternoon sun, rolling into Alabama to finish the second half of their mission. The trip, roughly seventy-five miles, took them about an hour and a half, mostly on two-lane roads. At the state line, Georgia 114 had turned into Alabama 68, and at Centre they turned onto Alabama 9, which would take them the rest of the way to Heflin.

They weren't far from their destination when Prentiss clicked her cell phone off. Even though Rossi and Carlyle only heard her side of the conversation, she could tell both men had been able to follow the conversation.

Rossi asked, "What was the victim's name?"

"Abigail Mathis," Prentiss said. "Actually, she was taken before the other two."

"From where?"

"Jesup, Georgia."

"Hell," Carlyle said. "That's the other side of the state—clear over by Savannah."

Rossi asked Prentiss, "Same timetable?"

"Less than a week before Heather Davison."

Rossi asked Carlyle, "How far is Jesup from Atlanta?"

With a slow shrug, the big African-American agent

said, "Two hundred thirty, maybe two hundred forty miles."

Prentiss said, "That's a long way from here."

Nodding, Rossi said, "Our UnSub's charted a pretty big hunting area. I'm thinking he started somewhere down that way, then came up here on his way north. He didn't just increase his hunting area, he moved. Maybe he was even on a spree as he headed north." He shook his head. "Still, there's got to be a way to narrow that area. It's time for a geographical profile."

Prentiss said, "Hotchner mentioned he had Reid doing one."

"Good."

"Hotch also said Abby Mathis was stolen from her house while she was asleep, and that her folks were asleep in the next room. Awfully bold."

Rossi made a sour face. "And another derivation."

Carlyle glanced a question at Rossi; then his eyes returned to the road.

Rossi said, "Anybody can make a bad decision and grab something that's out in the open—in this case, Heather Davison and Lee Ann Clark. Breaking into a house, that takes planning, that takes more than just *one* bad decision."

Prentiss said, "And look at it the other way around—going from planning an assault on a house to snatching victims of opportunity points to a spree, too."

"Yeah," Rossi said, eyebrows flicking up and down, "*if* there's a stressor in that area, around Savannah, that set him off. Might have caused the derivation."

Carlyle asked, "What kind of stressor?"

"That's what we need to find out," Rossi said. "Before we worry about that, though, let's get back to MO. When these kids disappeared, each was treated as a separate horrific crime, right?"

Carlyle nodded.

"Well, the cops in Summerville and Heflin had similar crimes, and not that much distance between them. They might well have compared notes, because they were looking for the same 'type' of criminal. Even though Jesup was only a week earlier, there would have been some synergy over the crimes, but, even just ten years ago, we didn't think there would be overlap in criminal types. We weren't nearly as adept at understanding the subtle link the victims play in crimes like these."

Prentiss said, "Three blonde girls of approximately the same age disappearing from two states."

"Right. Now we look for the similarities in the victims and why they were chosen over all the other three-year-old blonde girls in the same two-state area. Back then, we would have looked at the crime in Jesup and automatically assumed it was perpetrated by a different UnSub, because the only similarity to the other two crimes was that the victim was a blonde girl—everything else was different."

Prentiss, nodding, said, "That crime happened hundreds of miles away and was a break-in, while the others were children grabbed from public places."

Rossi shrugged. "At the time, we would have automatically assumed it was a coincidence."

Carlyle grunted. "I thought the manual said that we don't believe in coincidence."

"I absolutely don't believe in coincidence," Rossi said with a little chuckle, "except when one happens. Our problem now is to figure out this UnSub's signature in two kinds of crimes."

Carlyle said, "Hey, sorry, but I'm not following. You want me to just drive and shut up?"

"Hell no," Rossi said. "We can use the prodding. Let's start with MO—how our UnSub operates."

"Right."

"Assuming he's keeping these girls for that long a period of time, he's committing two types of crimes. First he kidnaps them, then much later he kills them. The MO on the three murders is exactly the same, nearly ritualistic."

"All right," Carlyle said, obviously getting it.

"But in the kidnappings, he's changed MOs— *why*?"

"No idea," Carlyle admitted.

"Something changed," Prentiss said. "That's the stressor Rossi mentioned."

"Okay," Carlyle said, "I can see that. . . ."

"Now," Rossi said, "here's the reason we're here. This UnSub also has a signature. It's not how he does the crime, it's what he *needs* to do for the crime, to give him what he's after."

"Girls," Carlyle said. "He needs girls."

"Not just any girls," Prentiss said.

"That's right," Rossi said. "Little girls, little *blonde* girls, toddlers, and why? And why those particular blonde girls over all the others in Georgia?"

Carlyle said, "Again, no idea."

"We don't know either," Rossi admitted, almost cheerfully. "But we will, we will."

The seat of Cleburne County, Heflin was home to 2,906 souls, according to the sign they passed as they rolled into town on Alabama 9 from the west. The highway turned into Ross Street and when they got to 405, Carlyle pulled into the parking lot of the Heflin Police Department.

Once inside, they repeated the process they'd gone through with Sheriff Burke up in Summerville. This time, their audience was a detective named Paul Wentworth, an athletic-looking young man in his early thirties with close-clipped brown hair, clear blue eyes and an easy smile. Dressed in jeans and a blue open-collar work shirt, Wentworth might well have been Rossi's son, and he paid respectful close attention as the senior FBI agent laid out what they had so far.

They were in a cramped office, Wentworth sitting on the corner of a messy desk looking down at Rossi and Prentiss in the visitors' chairs while Carlyle leaned on a file cabinet near the door.

"Am I right," Prentiss said, "in assuming you're too young to have worked on the original case?"

"That's right. It's fallen to me."

Rossi, his frustration evident (to Prentiss at least), asked, "Could we talk to the detective who worked the case?"

"Sorry, no—the investigating detective was a good cop, Clint Anderson." The young man's voice tightened with emotion. "We lost him to a heart attack, three years ago."

"Sorry," Rossi said. "This job can do that."

"Yes, it can," Wentworth said. He shifted gears. "I've read the file and I've even tried to dig around a little, but I'm afraid I haven't gotten anywhere."

They spoke for another ten minutes, but when they were finished, Prentiss hadn't learned a thing.

Wentworth led them across town, past the small park where Lee Ann had been abducted. This late in the day, school had been dismissed—with the temperature in the fifties, a few children were playing, wearing coats, playground equipment set off to one side, parents or babysitters sitting on nearby benches.

Prentiss figured when the abduction took place, the park would have been fairly crowded. A June day would have meant families with smaller children near the playground, older kids playing baseball, and traffic gliding by. Still, someone had been able to snatch Lee Ann Clark without being noticed.

As had been the case with Summerville, Prentiss figured the locals would likely have noticed a stranger. If the kidnapper was the same person who had grabbed Heather Davison, what state's plates were on the Aerostar?

Or was it possible that the kidnapper had changed

vehicles? Instead of helping build a profile, each crime scene seemed only to add questions. Were they getting closer or farther away from their quarry? She still did not know.

This neighborhood was only slightly more well-to-do than the Davisons' in Summerville. Like that block, very few cars were on the street; people were getting home from work now, so there was some traffic—but Prentiss would bet that most of these homes belonged to families where both parents worked and were away during the day.

The Clark home—a two-story clapboard house painted a faded maroon that almost looked like brick from a distance—had a gravel driveway that led to a new garage. Wentworth had phoned ahead, so they were expected. The local detective made the introductions at the front door, and then the Clarks invited the little group inside.

In a modest but immaculate living room, the Clarks shared a couch to the wall at the right; opposite, a flat-screen TV perched on a stand, electronic equipment on lower shelves. Potted plants covered a long table under the front picture window. No family photos were on display—no altar, this time, to a missing little girl. Several folding chairs were set up, waiting for their guests.

The three FBI agents took those while Wentworth occupied a wing chair next to the table of plants.

Prentiss didn't take long before profiling Brian and Michelle Clark as a kind, hardworking couple. Their son, five when his sister disappeared, had sprouted into a gangly teenager who made an appearance for introductions, then disappeared when his parents sat down to talk with the federal agents.

Like her deceased daughter, Michelle was a pretty blonde, with wavy tresses spilling down over her shoulders, bright brown eyes and porcelain skin. She wore jeans and a V-necked T-shirt with a small gold cross. Her husband—in a drab gray suit and dark tie, having just gotten home from work—was a broad-shouldered man with a blond crew cut and a guile-less expression belied by sharp blue eyes.

This meeting did not prove to spark the emotional devastation Prentiss had witnessed in the Davison home. Rather, the Clarks seemed almost relieved, fi-nally knowing they could surrender that final shred of hope of seeing their daughter alive again. Tears came, but relatively few.

"If we could," Rossi said, "we'd like to ask you a few questions."

The couple shared a look, then silently nodded consent. To Prentiss, they seemed of one mind—to survive their tragedy, a bond special even for a hus-band and wife had been formed.

Rossi said, "I know you've been over this again and again, but we need to hear it. So I'm afraid you're going to have to go through it one last time."

"We understand," Brian Clark said. He sighed, traded brave smiles with his pretty wife, then began: "We had taken the kids down to the park. It was a Saturday."

Abruptly, Rossi said, "Thank you for your time. We'll not intrude on you any longer."

"Thank you," Clark said.

His wife said the same thing.

Rising, Rossi said, "We're sorry for your loss, truly."

"Thank you," Clark repeated, rising as well.

The man of the house walked them outside. On the front porch, Rossi turned back to the grieving man. "Mr. Clark, for what it's worth, I'll tell you this—we'll do everything we can to catch whoever did this to your daughter."

"I saw you on TV."

Rossi blinked, as this momentarily felt like a non sequitur. "Yes . . . I wrote some books."

"I read one of them. I believe Michelle and I are lucky to have you on the case."

"Thank you. But I can assure you that everyone on my team is the best the FBI has to offer. Again, for what that's worth."

When Clark went back inside the house, the agents bade farewell to Detective Wentworth and thanked him for his assistance. Rossi promised to keep him informed.

On the road, heading back to Atlanta, Prentiss said, "You ended that pretty quickly."

Shrugging with one shoulder, Rossi turned to her in the backseat. "That half hour they spent searching for their daughter gave the UnSub a thirty-minute head start getting out of town. You figure the local police wasted another hour or more searching around town. Even if the locals called the state police as soon as the Clarks called them, the UnSub still had over a thirty-minute lead. Everything that happened in Heflin after the girl disappeared was about chasing a ghost. The UnSub was long gone."

Carlyle asked, "Do you think the UnSub picked them because they were new in town?"

"Maybe," Rossi said. "But more likely, pure dumb luck. Otherwise, he drove across Georgia into Alabama, to case this particular park? Very doubtful. I think this whole series of crimes started even before the kidnapping in Jesup. That one was planned. These other two, why come clear across the state to stalk families over here? No, this was part of a spree."

"What's next?" Carlyle asked, but Prentiss already knew.

"Tomorrow," Rossi said, "we'll go to Jesup. The beginning is there, and the beginning always holds the answer."

Chapter Six

Hibbing, Minnesota

He was in Hibbing on business, which also gave him time to start shopping for the perfect present to keep His Beloved happy. She had been sad for months, His Beloved, ever since Paula left for finishing school, and now the time had come to start anew.

When he'd last gone shopping, the world had been a different, more innocent place. Now there were AMBER Alerts, video cameras everywhere, and the Internet to contend with. Things moved at a much faster pace and on such a larger scale—how he longed for simpler times.

And if he slipped up, they would never have a family to love and nurture again.

He would be gone overnight. With good planning and a little luck, he could go shopping today, and pick up His Beloved's present tomorrow, on the way out of town.

The woman he adored needed children as much as oxygen. She had such a large capacity for love, and when there was no one to share it with—except for him, of course, and he wasn't able to fill the depths of her needs—the melancholy leached into her system and seemed to suck at her soul, like a ravenous beast. This he had learned long ago. But his love for her was so great, he only wanted her to be happy, and would do anything to fulfill her needs.

She was scarred from a childhood of verbal abuse that had become something far worse, once she was old enough to (as her father had so crudely put it) "go on the rag."

He was appalled by how terrible some people could be—and the man had been her *father!*

Her mother had been almost as bad, taking His Beloved to a back-alley abortionist who'd butchered the job so badly that she could never have children of her own. Unlike the horrible father, though, the mother might have felt some small measure of guilt, eventually killing herself with sleeping pills. Later, His Beloved's father had been killed when his shotgun had mysteriously discharged while he was cleaning it—a terrible thing for a young girl to have to witness.

She had run away then, His Beloved, and lived on her own briefly, doing whatever she could to survive, until he had met her—"My little knight in shiny armor," she called him. They had fallen in love on their very first date and been together ever since. On their way east from his college graduation, headed to his first job, they had stopped for their first "shopping trip."

She had been wearing him down for months with talk of how easy it would be for them to find a child, a nice blonde girl, like herself, and how much happier they would be with kids in the house. With so many terrible parents out there, giving a really good home to a child would be a blessing for all concerned. Finally, on that trip, he had given in.

A doting mother, His Beloved cherished the children until that dreaded time when they would reach that "special" age. She trusted no men at all, except him of course, although in this one area, he could not convince her that he would never, ever consider doing what that monster of a father had done to her. She would imitate her father's deep voice, mimicking one of the terrible things she'd heard him say: "Old enough to bleed, old enough to breed!"

His Beloved knew she was scarred—she was nothing if not self-aware—and had seen several shrinks along the way, to try to ease her pain. Mostly, their solutions had involved pills—pills she took to control nearly every aspect of her life: anxiety, depression, mood swings, and, of course, sleep. The nightmares were the worst but the sleeping pills allowed her some peace and seemed to keep her dream demons battered back into their cave. These pills also came in handy when the time came to send their precious girls off to finishing school.

The first girl had been sent to finishing school while he was away at work one day. If he had been home, he would have tried to prevent it; she knew it, he knew it, so His Beloved simply waited for him to leave for work one morning, then made the girl a good-bye breakfast.

Unable to face losing His Beloved, and knowing there was no way to tell anyone—they had adopted the child through decidedly unofficial means that the authorities, indeed society at large, would neither understand nor condone—he had remained silent.

That had been difficult.

But not any more difficult than going shopping had been, when he'd had to come to terms with the price of making His Beloved happy, which was to deprive some other mother and father of their child. That part, however, had become more and more easy to cope with when he had seen how good a mother His Beloved was. She was the best, most nurturing mother on God's green earth. Thinking about it now, sitting in his rental car, he knew that they had done the right thing. Those girls had been so much better off with the two of them than the neglectful parents who had turned their backs and made it possible for him to retrieve the children. After all, if they had been good parents, they never would have made it so easy for him to go shopping.

He was parked near a day care center on East Twenty-fifth Street, tucked where no one could easily see him in the parking lot of Vic Power Park. With his binoculars, he could sit in the car and easily see who came and went from the day care center.

That presented a tiny risk—someone might notice the binoculars and get suspicious; but this November afternoon was passing on the wings of a harsh north wind that kept traffic to a minimum. The park, except for two high school kids on the far side who had apparently skipped afternoon classes to hang out and smoke, was vacant. The two teens wanted nothing to do with the adult in the big blue car. They not only kept their distance, but they kept their backs to him, more worried that he would recognize them than the other way around.

Didn't take long for the children to parade out, their parents picking them up and leading them to cars parked along the street. Not long after dismissal, he saw what he was looking for, and she was perfect—perky and blonde, with a smile so wide that he knew His Beloved would fall in love at first sight with the child. Normally he was not an impulse buyer, but this time he knew at once that he didn't have to shop any further.

She was so gorgeous in her jeans, sneakers, and little pink parka zipped to her neck, a Bratz backpack slung over one shoulder as she toddled over to meet a woman, presumably her mother, who also wore jeans, sneakers, and a parka, though the woman's coat was purple, with a Minnesota Vikings logo on the back. She, too, was blonde and slim. Were she here, His Beloved would be jealous of the way his eyes relished the mother as she held the hand of the little girl and led her to a black Lincoln Navigator parked at the curb.

After the girl was strapped into her car seat, the mother climbed aboard, started the vehicle and merged into the eastbound traffic on East Twenty-fifth. He had set aside the binoculars while the little girl was being tucked into her seat. When the Lincoln pulled out, his car was already started and he put two cars between his and the black Navigator. He was pretty sure the woman had not noticed him, but then hardly anyone ever noticed him, in or out of a car. Still, no point in tailgating—wasn't like he was some simple brigand getting ready to carjack her. This took an element of . . . grace.

He stayed well back as Twenty-fifth changed into Dupont Road. East of town, where North Dublin Road ran south to the airport, she crossed eastward, the road changing names yet again, becoming Lake Carey Road. He was having more trouble now. He had to lag back as the cars between them had all turned off. Following too close might spook the mother and that was the last thing he needed.

As the road turned north, to loop around Lake Carey, he stayed far enough back that she was occasionally out of sight for a second or two. When he came around a corner and she wasn't there, he blurted, "Darn!" Then, off to the right, he saw tail-lights blink on in the garage of a log-cabin-type house, and recognized the Navigator before the electric garage door started down.

All right—that was home.

His options seemed limited—attaining the child on the route home seemed impossible; equally hard would be trying to get the girl *at* home. Darkness was settling in, the days getting short fast this far north. That left the day care as the most vulnerable spot. He would follow them from the house tomorrow, just in case, but he expected the retrieval would happen at the day care.

That meant he had a lot of planning to do between now and tomorrow.

Which was fine. He would do anything for His Beloved. And anything worth doing was worth doing right.

Bemidji, Minnesota

Frustration was an emotion with which Dr. Spencer Reid was of course familiar, but rarely in his work, which was after all his refuge.

Dealing with his schizophrenic mother had obviously been, and continued to be, a frustrating experience—she was still housed in the Bennington Sanitarium in their hometown of Las Vegas. Being eighteen years old and forced to deal with his mother's illness had matured him fast (Reid's father had been MIA since the young man's youth). He had been among older kids from very early on, jumping grades, graduating from high school at twelve, always doing his best to seem older than his age.

But the truth was, he'd always felt younger than

his age, until the day his mother had been committed, anyway. That day, at eighteen, he'd been a man. He had to be.

Even with all his extensive reading, his three doctoral degrees, and the benefit of an IQ of 187, he had still not been able to help his mother. That frustration had never been quelled. Work helped him hold his frustration at bay—usually.

This particular case, however, was frustration squared, holding a plethora of suspects who fit different aspects of their profile, but none fitting *every* aspect of the profile. Did this mean the BAU team was on the right track, just not quite there? Or did it mean their profile was wrongly skewed?

Another question nagged at Reid—had they overlooked a suspect, while centering in on Billy Rohl and the other members of the hunting party?

He recalled sylviculturist Lawrence Silvan saying several inspectors spent a good deal of time in that forest. The profilers should probably be interviewing those inspectors, both as suspects and possible witnesses. Though the UnSub was clearly careful, one of the inspectors might have seen something, and not realized its significance.

After running this past Hotchner and Morgan, Reid got out Silvan's card and phoned the cell number on the back. With evening settling over Bemidji, Reid did not expect to find the forester in the office. He was wrong.

Silvan answered on the first ring. "Lawrence Silvan."

"Mr. Silvan, this is Dr. Spencer Reid, with the FBI?"

"Yes, Dr. Reid, I remember. How can I help you?"

"When we spoke yesterday, you told us forest number four had more than one inspector—am I remembering correctly?" Of course, he knew he was.

"Yes, three of us, on a rotating basis."

"May I have their names and contact information?"

Silvan complied: The other inspectors were Randy Beck and Jason Fryman. Phone numbers and home addresses were provided as well.

"Thank you, sir. Can you also come in for an interview?"

"Well, certainly, Dr. Reid. But you must understand that we all travel extensively. I doubt any of us could get in before Friday—although if you're going to be at the law enforcement center at this time tomorrow night, I might make it."

"Let's say Friday morning, then," Reid said. "Thanks for your help."

They signed off, and Reid set about getting Fryman and Beck in for interviews. Both men agreed to come in first thing Friday morning. With that done, Reid thought about calling it a day. He was tired, frustrated, and wondering where to turn next when Hotchner said, "The crime lab guy is on his way back with Garue."

Reid and Morgan managed to pull themselves up a little straighter in their chairs and JJ, who seemed impervious to long hours, simply pulled her chair a little closer to the others.

The Native American detective entered, his gray hair hanging lank; he looked as fatigued as Reid felt. With Garue was a tall, muscular man with close-cropped brown hair, a wide forehead, tight brown eyes, and a face that looked like it doled out smiles only sparingly.

Garue introduced the agents, then said, "This is Fletcher Keegan from the regional office of the Minnesota Bureau of Criminal Apprehension."

Eyeing the big man, who wore work boots, jeans, and (beneath a Windbreaker) a navy Polo shirt with the state BCA logo, Reid had a feeling of déjà vu.

He said, "We've met before, Mr. Keegan."

Keegan managed a twitch of a smile. "I didn't think you'd remember, Dr. Reid," he said, his voice a rich baritone. "You sat in on a lecture Jason Gideon gave when I attended the National Academy."

"That's right," Reid said. "And you know Rossi."

Nodding, Keegan said, "I do, but I notice he's not here."

Hotchner said, "When we got word about the victims having originally been abducted in the South, Rossi and SSA Prentiss went down there to investigate from that end."

"Good idea," Keegan said. "But maybe I have some information that will help you at this end."

"Glad to hear it."

Hotchner gestured for the man to sit, and he did, the team leader, too. Garue followed suit.

"First," Keegan said, "now that we've had more time to study the bodies, we can state with surety that the girls were all in good health at the time of their murders."

Hotchner frowned. "Could you define 'good health' more precisely?"

"Certainly. Good health as in not so much as a cavity among the three of them. Their teeth were perfect. One would have benefited from some orthodontic work, but her teeth were healthy and strong. Just as the others' were."

"Which tells you what?"

"The UnSub fed them well. You would have to say he nourished them. None had so much as a broken fingernail. For lack of a better phrase, if I can wander into your territory of profiling . . . ?"

"Be our guest."

"Well, he loved them. That's what has me stymied." Keegan shrugged, shook his head. "I could find *no* sign that these girls had been mistreated in any way before they were killed."

With the tiniest of smiles, Hotchner asked, "What did you learn about kidnapping at the National Academy?"

Keegan didn't hesitate: "Three reasons to kidnap: profit, sexual deviance, and to obtain a child an UnSub could not otherwise have."

Morgan said, "And we have no ransom notes."

Keegan nodded, and said, "And no signs of sexual abuse that I could find."

Hotchner said, "That means our UnSub was looking for some other kind of fulfillment from the crime. What was it?"

Keegan shrugged and said, "I've already wandered too far into your territory."

"No idea," Garue said, shaking his head.

Hotchner's expression was grave, even for him. "We need to find out two things to catch this UnSub—why he took these children, and what went wrong with his situation."

Keegan said, "How do we know something 'went wrong with his situation'?"

Reid said, "He held three girls from three different abductions for ten years, then suddenly decided that they needed to die."

Hotchner picked up the thread: "But not all at once—over a period of a year. Did they somehow become a threat to him after all that time?"

Morgan, frowning, said, "Ten years, and they're suddenly a threat? Why?"

"I don't know," Hotchner admitted. "But if we figure it out, we'll understand the UnSub. Then we can catch him."

"There's another thing," Keegan said, lifting a hand like a student in class. "About the girls' clothes . . . ?"

"What?" Morgan asked.

"They were all homemade. We thought, at first, that maybe the tags had just been cut out, but closer inspection indicated they were in fact homemade."

Hotchner asked, "What about the cloth?"

"Common stuff sold in any number of fabric-and-yarn shops within a thousand miles." Keegan shrugged. "I don't know if it helps or not, knowing that."

"It definitely helps," Reid said. "It helps by bringing up more questions."

Keegan frowned. "More questions is a *good* thing?"

"In profiling it is. Are homemade clothes a reflection of the economic status of our UnSub? Or were the clothes homemade because the UnSub didn't want anyone to know he had children? Obviously, the girls weren't in the public school system."

"Or any private school we can find," Garue added.

Reid continued, in a rush of words. "They were likely homeschooled, if the UnSub even bothered with that. But with the homemade clothes, are they the signs that the UnSub has a wife? Or is the UnSub female? Does a male UnSub have the sewing skills to make those clothes? Is that an insight into his employment?"

Holding up a hand, Hotchner said, "That's enough questions for the moment—let's get back at it and start finding some answers."

Hibbing, Minnesota

The overcast morning sky held the promise of a coming storm, which could not help but remind him of his own situation. Although the plan for their impending departure had been taking shape since the burial of Paula, he could clearly see the pace would have to increase.

His Beloved had ordered enough meds to facilitate sending the girls to finishing school, as well as covering her own needs should they require a hasty departure. That possibility existed, he knew. The finding of the graves by those nosy hunters had been both unforeseen and unfortunate. Though the possibility of discovery always loomed, he had not counted on hunters simply stumbling onto the girls, especially not so soon.

He now realized that if today's shopping trip was unsuccessful, they might well have to complete their new family on the fly—not the first time, but hardly ideal, meaning less chance of him putting together the perfect family for His Beloved.

He had a vague belief in omens, however, and the heavy cloud cover of the morning provided just the sort of tiny advantage that could make all the difference. He certainly didn't want to do this on a bright, sunny day if he could avoid it, and the cobalt sky made his job, at least slightly, easier. And if God had been against what he planned, wouldn't the Almighty have stuck him with sunshine?

He pulled into a long, tree-lined lane and turned around, then parked just out of sight of anybody driving along Lake Carey Road. He hoped the perfect child would be along soon and he would just fall in behind her. The last thing he needed was whoever lived at the other end of the lane pulling up behind him to ask what the heck he was up to.

As he waited, he tried to come up with a legitimate excuse to be sitting in the private drive of someone he did not know. He got out his cell phone and rested it on the passenger seat. If he saw a vehicle in his rearview, he would put it up to his ear and claim that he had pulled off to take an important call—a quasi-believable excuse.

If the darn mother would just drive by with that beautiful child, he could get the heck out of here and stop worrying about maybes and might-bes and could-bes. Wasn't like he didn't have enough on his mind already! Assuming the mother simply mirrored her route home last night, he would follow her to the day care, then wait for everything to settle down, so he could enact the plan that he had worked on most of last night.

He had driven back past the house yesternight, gotten the last name off the roadside mailbox, then gone back to his room and got online on his laptop. Took some digging, but he now knew a great deal more about the Scheckel family. His plan was less than masterful, he knew, but better than nothing.

At least he had a shot.

He was hoping, though, that he might find his chance before little Marie—a name he had learned from the family's own home page—was locked up inside the day care center.

He glanced in the rearview mirror, and once again heaved a sigh of relief when he saw nothing. Looking out toward the road, he willed the black Navigator to appear.

It did.

Thank you, God, he thought, sitting numbly as the vehicle rolled by.

He was so surprised that the SUV had shown up the moment he had willed it, he almost didn't put his car into gear to follow. When he finally dropped the gearshift into drive, he was well behind the Navigator. The morning traffic picked up more as they neared town. The street name turned back from Lake Carey Road to Dupont when they crossed North Dublin. He was closer now, following along, just another commuter heading to work.

When Dupont Road turned into Twenty-fifth Street, he got a nagging notion that his shopping trip might end in frustration. He stayed with the SUV, but something told him he should just give up. He had listened to his inner voice on more than one occasion and found his intuition to be trustworthy.

He decided he would follow her to the day care and then would watch the little girl go inside and out of his life, a missed opportunity for them both. The more he considered his plan, the less likely success seemed. He had hoped to present himself as an operative of a security company hired by the family. He had an old badge he'd swiped from a rent-a-cop nearly twenty years ago. Sometimes, in an emergency, such a ploy could work, but he didn't like the way this felt. He was getting a vibe that something was . . . off.

Then, as if he been granted another break by God, he noticed the Navigator's left blinker coming on blocks short of the day care.

What was Mommy up to?

Looking to where she was turning, he saw a convenience store with parking places near the building, gas pumps nearer the street. The lot butted up against a restaurant that came to the sidewalk, the parking lot on the east side, the convenience store to the west beyond the eatery.

The restaurant was one of those steak places that didn't open until late afternoon, and he had a sudden idea. Instead of following the Navigator into the convenience store lot, he jerked the wheel and turned left into the restaurant's. He parked on the east side of the building, then jumped out of the car and walked briskly but inconspicuously, around the restaurant toward the convenience store. He stopped short when he saw Mommy pumping gas, the little girl still strapped into her car seat in the back.

The convenience store's front windows allowed him to see most of the action inside. One guy paid for coffee at the cash register, near the door. The guy came out, climbed into a white car and pulled out the side entrance to the west.

Still watching, he pretended to bend down to tie a shoe while he searched for the surveillance cameras. The restaurant had none—a staid old steak house that didn't worry about its parking lot. The convenience store, on the other hand, would be trying to catch drive-offs. They might have cameras everywhere.

In the end, he counted four, all mounted on the flat roof of the store, all pointed toward the pumps. A fifth camera, and maybe a sixth and seventh as well, would be inside; but he didn't care about those—they'd be focused on the front door, the register area, and, if the owner was exceptionally paranoid, the beer coolers.

Making sure he stayed behind the woman, he waited. If she paid at the pump, he was wasting his time. If she went inside to pay, he had one chance.

When she replaced the pump nozzle, he figured he was out of luck. She leaned into the vehicle's driver door and he assumed she had paid at the pump, using her card while he had hotfooted it around the restaurant. Shaking his head, knowing now that the bad vibe had been right, he shoved his hands in the pockets of his jacket. As he was about to turn back to the car, the mother leaned back out of the SUV and closed the door. Holding bills in her gloved hand, she turned toward him.

He willed himself to be invisible and she continued toward the store. He could not believe his luck. The lot was empty, except for the Navigator and a car parked near the door that probably belonged to the employee inside. At this time of the morning, more people should be around, picking up coffee, newspapers, energy drinks, and doughnuts.

Yet, as he approached the SUV, careful to stay on the sidewalk as though he were just walking past, his chin tucked into his chest, his eyes to his left watching the woman go into the store, he could only smile. No one was out here but him and her. Another sign that God was on his side . . .

When the woman went past the counter and back to the coffee station, he knew the time to take his shot had come. Easing up to the SUV's back door, he kept his eyes on the clerk, who was talking to the woman—maybe she was a regular.

Heart pounding now, he touched the back door handle—unlocked. The door opened as if he and it were old friends. His chest pounded, his heart banging against his ribs, as if trying to make a break for it. When he finally tore his eyes away from the two people in the store, he looked into the ocean-blue eyes of the girl in her car seat.

She smiled at him.

"Hiiiii," she said, her voice tiny, but warm.

"Hi," he said back. Already hurriedly unstrapping her, he said, "You want to go see your mommy?"

She nodded. "I wanna doughnut."

"We'll go get you one," he said, eyes cutting to the woman inside as she put the lid on her coffee. She was about to turn back toward the front of the store. He needed to be gone.

He slipped the girl out of the car seat and took off at a run, barely getting the SUV door shut before he tore off. That one thing, the closed door of the Lincoln, with the illusion that all was well, might buy him the few extra seconds he needed.

Not looking back now, the girl holding tight to his chest, too surprised even to cry out, he sprinted around the corner of the restaurant, cars on the street and possible witnesses be darned as he bounced along, struggling to get his keys out of his coat pocket and control the girl at the same time.

"Hey!" she said, realizing something was wrong.

He fumbled at the lock once, twice, three times, silently cursing, his heart sure to explode in his chest now. Finally, the key fit into the lock.

"I wan' my mommy!"

"Patience, dear," he said.

He twisted the key, threw open the door and put the girl on the front seat.

"Mommy!" the girl screamed, but the slamming car door swallowed the sound. He ran around and heaved the driver's door open, dove in, cranked the car to life, and tried to pull away smoothly.

The girl was crying on the seat next to him now, still too stunned to do anything but wail. Turning right, he pulled onto Twenty-fifth and melted into traffic. As he looked in the rearview mirror, he saw the hysterical woman looking this way and that on the street, wondering what had become of her daughter.

Careless bitch.

Timing was everything now. He had to assume someone had seen the rental car, if not him and the girl. He sped across Twenty-fifth, but not *too* fast.

He reminded himself of a lesson he had learned a long time ago—never commit a misdemeanor while committing a felony.

At the corner of North Dublin Road, he took the right and headed south for the Chisholm-Hibbing Airport. Driving south, the little girl louder now, he saw a cop coming the opposite way and, for a moment, his breath caught. He watched the black-and-white for a long time, until it disappeared from the side mirror. Then, finally, he took another breath.

As the little girl became harder and harder to control while he drove, he became convinced he'd need to move to step two, soon. He pulled into the parking lot of a closed tavern, got out of the car, went around to the trunk and removed the chloroform from his bag. After splashing a little on the handkerchief, he closed the trunk, then went to the front and opened the door.

The little girl screamed.

He put the rag over her nose and mouth and she stopped screaming.

He threw the handkerchief into a nearby trash can. He got back into the car and got back onto the road. He hadn't wanted to stop before the airport and now the fear was spiking in him again. Still, he forced himself not to drive too fast.

He pulled into the airport, half surprised not to see any cops. He pulled up behind his own car and stopped. First, he took his bag from the trunk of the rental and put it into his trunk. Next, after carefully checking for other people in the parking lot, he retrieved the slumbering child and put her in the car seat he had waiting for her, and strapped her up.

Safety first.

Pulse pounding, sweat beading on his brow, he climbed in and started the car, backed out of the parking place, and pulled away. By the time he was half an hour out of Hibbing, looking over at the little Sleeping Beauty, his fear had been replaced by elation.

He had done it.

He had the perfect present for His Beloved and he just couldn't wait to show her.

Chapter Seven

Jesup, Georgia

They had left Atlanta early, before eight, and gotten caught up in rush hour traffic. Special Agent Scotty Carlyle once again drove the SUV with Rossi riding shotgun and Prentiss in back. The trip was 230 miles and Rossi had planned on four hours, letting them get to Jesup before lunch. The Atlanta traffic had killed that idea before they were even out of town.

Carlyle had taken I-75 south out of town. Eighty miles later, where I-475 veered south around Macon and hooked up with I-75S again, Carlyle stayed on his easterly route that became I-16E headed for Savannah.

At Dublin, Carlyle cut south again, taking U.S. 331 to McRae and then turning onto U.S. 341 for the last long easterly leg of the trip to Jesup. As they entered Wayne County, they were greeted by a sign that read SOUTHEAST GEORGIA'S BEST KEPT SECRET. Rossi hoped that wasn't true, at least as far as their investigation was concerned. When they got into Jesup, Carlyle took a right onto Sunset Boulevard.

"All right, Mr. DeMille," Rossi said, "I'm ready for my close-up."

"Say what?" Carlyle asked.

Prentiss said, "You've never seen *Sunset Boulevard*? Classic film? Billy Wilder?"

Glancing over, Carlyle asked, "Any brothers in it?"

"No," Rossi said, with half a smile, "just William Holden and Gloria Swanson."

"Never heard of it." Then, tapping himself on the chest, Carlyle said, " 'I *am* big—it's the *pictures* that got small.' "

Rossi and Prentiss laughed.

Carlyle said, "You think the only movies I ever saw had Fred Williamson in 'em?"

Rossi shook his head. "Just figured you were too damn young."

"Maybe so," Carlyle said, "but I took a film class when I was an undergrad at Ball State. And, anyway, Turner Classic Movies comes with basic cable."

From Sunset Boulevard, Carlyle made the left onto Orange Street and rolled into downtown Jesup, though that was a grandiose way to put it for this home to a shade over ten thousand people. The business district had a small-town feel with mom-and-pop businesses interspersed with occasional vacant storefronts.

Soon they were pulling up across the street from a newish-looking brick building with the words JESUP POLICE DEPARTMENT in granite above the door, to the left of which was a picture window bearing the department's logo.

They parked and got out, Rossi noticing no meters

to feed. People on sidewalks on either side were split between those who ignored the visitors and others who frankly studied with good-natured suspicion the strangers with the government plates on their vehicle. As the trio of FBI agents crossed in the middle of the block, a pickup driven by a greasy-haired young man slowed down for him to eyeball them.

A wooden bench under the big window of the police station was the current location of a lanky African-American in a gray suit and an open-collar white shirt, eating a candy bar, as if to bulk up some. With his short black hair and a full goatee, he probably appeared older than he was, and Rossi made him for no more than thirty. His warm brown eyes brightened and he smiled and rose as they neared.

"Detective Tim Mickerson," he said, extending his hand.

Carlyle shook the man's hand and made the introductions.

Mickerson squinted and put on a sideways grin. "Not the *writer* David Rossi?"

"Guilty as charged," Rossi said with a nod. "About ten years ago, the White Sox had a bonus baby named Mickerson, I believe."

The detective's grin straightened. "Also guilty. A Sox fan?"

"Baseball fan," Rossi said. "Cubs, though."

Mickerson made a face. "Dirty job, but I guess somebody's gotta do it."

"That doesn't mean I don't appreciate talent. Are you the Mickerson in question?"

"Yeah," Mickerson said, trying to rotate his shoulder. "And a baby no more—not after a torn labrum. Damn thing never healed right. I came back here and became a cop."

Rossi said, "Nothing wrong with that, except the paycheck."

Shrugging, the detective said, "Hey, cost of living's low down here, and I like the work just fine. It's not baseball, but I've still got a little nest egg."

"A lot of guys don't," Rossi said, shaking his head. "Sign a ball for me?"

"For a Cubs fan?" Mickerson asked, rubbing his chin. "Maybe, if the famous writer signed a book for me . . ."

"We could do a trade," Rossi said with a grin, and the two men shook on it.

"Now," Mickerson said, the candy bar wrapper disappearing into a jacket pocket, "let's talk about why you're here."

Prentiss said, "Abigail Mathis."

Mickerson's expression went sober. "June 1998. Biggest crime this town ever saw."

Rossi asked, "Were you here yet?"

"Naw. Still playin' ball back then. I'll introduce you to Malcolm Henry—he was the investigator then, retired now. So, you want to meet the family first or look at the evidence?"

"Well, we're here," Rossi said, glancing at the police station. "Let's look at the evidence."

Mickerson reached in an inside jacket pocket and

withdrew a folded piece of paper. He unfolded it and handed it over to Rossi.

Rossi studied the photograph of a boot print in the mud. "What's this?"

"That's the evidence," Mickerson said. "Unless you want the window screen the killer cut. He cut it with a serrated knife."

Prentiss said, "He wasn't a killer then."

Shrugging, Mickerson said, "He is now."

"Well," Rossi said, "now that we've gone over the evidence, let's meet the family."

As they rode along—Mickerson up front navigating, as Carlyle drove, Rossi now in the back with Prentiss—the senior profiler couldn't help but think about the number of people this case had touched. Not just the three victims, but their parents, family and friends, and God only knew who else. He'd seen some of these monsters get famous, sometimes in part because of him, while their many victims (a list not limited to just the actual murder victims) languished in anonymity.

It stunk.

He had made calls on victims' families many times in the old days. Although he had come back to the BAU for his own reasons, he wondered how much longer he could continue to immerse himself in the rivers of despair these human monsters created, and not come away as broken as Jason Gideon or Max Ryan or Elle Greenaway. The latter he didn't know, but he had heard—Prentiss was her replacement.

The profilers all guarded themselves against burnout as best they could; still, the threat was always there. Other personal damage could be inflicted by the job, like the marital trouble that had crept up on Hotchner, who in part saw himself as fighting for all families like his and along the way lost his wife and was now struggling to maintain a decent relationship with his son. Chalk up another family ripped apart by these monsters.

The Mathises lived in a rambling story-and-a-half clapboard on Charleston Street, west and a little south of the police station. The white house looked like every other house on the block. The driveway might be on the other side here and there, and one yard's tree might be taller than another's, but essentially the house and yard were interchangeable with their neighbors.

Somehow, out of this sameness, the UnSub had chosen the little girl who perfectly fit his psychotic need.

How?

Why?

At the front door of the house, Mickerson made the introductions and the agents were invited inside. The living room of the Mathis home was small and devoid of family photos of any kind.

No television in the room, either, the furnishings plain, simple—a gray couch against one wall, two chairs divided by a picture window, a midroom plain brown table bearing the day's neatly folded newspaper and a Bible. No magazines, no electronic devices,

not so much as a cell phone set down anywhere—
the electric lamps on the sofa's end tables seemed the
family's only acquiescence to modern technology.

Blond, blue-eyed Ansen Mathis would not have
been out of place on a recruiting poster for the
Aryan Nation, with his wide shoulders and muscular arms. Mathis—in a denim jacket over a navy
blue T-shirt and jeans—had pale skin for such a
sunny clime, and a smile as narrow and straight as
a razor slash.

His wife, Ashley, had shoulder-length blonde hair,
green eyes, a rosy complexion and a slender build.
She wore a lightweight brown jacket over a scoop-
neck blue shirt. She too wore jeans. They looked to
Rossi like a countrified version of the bride and
groom from atop a wedding cake.

The Mathises each took a chair, the picture window between them, while the three federal agents
squeezed onto the small couch and Mickerson remained standing.

At least Rossi had been spared the notification job
this time—the family had been informed of their
daughter's death as soon as she was identified. But
judging from the somber expressions and red-
rimmed eyes of Ansen and Ashley Mathis, the
wound remained raw.

When everyone had settled, Rossi met Mathis's
blue eyes. "Tell us about that day, sir, if you're up
to it."

Mathis let out a long breath. "That night was like
any other, I'd have to say. We read Abby a story,

kissed her good night, and went to bed ourselves. Wasn't till we got up, next morning, we realized she was gone. Ashley called 911 right away, and I went door to door in the neighborhood, but it was too late."

Rossi nodded politely. Mrs. Mathis was using a tissue to dab at tears.

"I wonder if we could back up," Prentiss said, sitting forward. "Could we hear about your *whole* day that day?"

Ansen and Ashley Mathis traded a confused look.

"You can widen that," Rossi said, "to the several days before."

Bewildered, Mathis asked, "Why, Agent Rossi?"

Rossi sighed. "The Unknown Subject who abducted your daughter did not pick her at random. As I believe you were informed, this individual has abducted other children, all of whom share your daughter's basic description. So a little dark-haired girl down the block wouldn't do, and neither would a redheaded boy or girl two streets over. Whoever took Abby did so because she fit his unique needs . . . and because he knew she would be here—here, in *this* house, not any of the other houses in this neighborhood. So the question I come up with, as an investigator, is: How did he know which house the blonde girl lived in?"

Mrs. Mathis shrugged and her husband frowned in thought.

Rossi said, "I know you went over all this, time and again, ten years ago. But if there's something . . ."

No one said anything for a long moment.

He tried again: "Whoever took your child knew where to look—and we just have to figure out *how* he knew."

"I'm sorry," Mathis said, wide-eyed, shaking his head. "But other than our friends at church, we hardly see anybody. We keep to ourselves and a small circle."

Prentiss asked, "Did Abby go to preschool?"

Mrs. Mathis said, "Yes—at the church."

Rossi asked, "Which church?"

Mathis said, "New Kingdom Worship Church."

"How long have you been members?"

"Twenty years for me," Mrs. Mathis said. "A couple years less for Ansen."

Rossi asked, "Is the membership steady, or is there turnover? Do people come and go?"

Mathis allowed some teeth to show through the razor-blade smile. "Not a lot of turnover *anywhere* in Jesup, Mr. Rossi. I bet we haven't lost five families at our church in all the time we've been there."

Rossi asked them more questions, including whether they'd seen any out-of-state vehicles or suspicious individuals near the house or even just in town, but neither parent could come up with anything.

Finally Rossi nodded. "Thank you for your time—and we are truly sorry for your loss."

"Thank you," Mathis said. "And God bless you."

"God bless you," his wife said.

Coming from these two, the words were not a rote

farewell; Rossi sensed the genuine depth of their thanks for the law enforcers' efforts.

Outside, Rossi said, "We need to check out that church. Who left and when they left. For now, though, let's go talk with your detective. Excuse me, what was his name?"

"Malcolm Henry," Mickerson said.

"Let's go meet Detective Henry."

Bemidji, Minnesota

The team had come in early this morning and had already been hard at work for several hours when Special Agent in Charge Aaron Hotchner got himself a cup of coffee from the break room. When Hotchner returned to the conference room, he found Reid poring over maps trying to put together a geographic profile. Morgan was on the laptop with Garcia, the two going over the backgrounds of their suspects against the pieces of the profile that were slowly falling into place, like a jigsaw puzzle assembling itself in slow motion.

The BAU members didn't know much, admittedly; but they were sure of a few things.

The UnSub was comfortable in the woods.

On the other hand, he was uncomfortable with confrontation.

He was nonviolent, in his way, despite being a murderer. (Those two facts Hotchner had gleaned from the UnSub poisoning his victims.)

Seemed to be no sign of hatred or anger in his murders.

The use of poison also made Hotchner think that the UnSub was not only uncomfortable with confrontation, but with people in general. This was a person who would avoid confrontation at all cost as well as try to not interact with people any more than necessary.

Hotchner further figured that the UnSub would have a job that would minimize contact with people. That did not, however, make Hotchner believe that the killer might not try to insinuate himself into the investigation to try to find out what the police knew.

Some serial killers would inject themselves into an investigation to gain a feeling of power from being close to the police and knowing that the very people tracking him were unaware of his nearby presence. This UnSub, however, would insinuate himself strictly for intelligence gathering.

The UnSub was smart. The use of barbiturates required at least some education to give the correct dosage, including providing an overdose. If he merely made the victim sick, or gave the victim too severe a dosage, that person might grow suspicious or even vomit. And he would fail.

As both a kidnapper and murderer, the UnSub was highly organized. No one had seen anything of him at any of the crime scenes, and after three abductions, three murders, and three burials, no witnesses at all had come forward. The UnSub had cased at least the first victim of what appeared to be a kidnapping spree.

Granted, the environment had been different when the UnSub started, no AMBER Alerts and the like; but still the UnSub had managed to abduct three girls in a relatively small area, then disappeared for ten years. No small feat, Hotchner allowed.

The more Hotchner thought about it, the more likely it seemed they might well be dealing with multiple UnSubs. A female seemed out of the question, simply because the girls were buried deeper into the woods than a normal-sized woman could possibly have carried them. The lack of witnesses of any kind indicated the UnSub had the ability to be all but invisible.

Since a normal-sized woman could not have carried the girls so far from the road—and since a larger woman probably would have been noticed somewhere along the line—to Hotchner it seemed highly improbable that the UnSub was female.

Which did not mean that the UnSub was a man. That is, the unlikelihood of the UnSub being a woman did not mean that a man *and* a woman weren't involved in this together. They might be, as Reid had surmised, dealing with accomplices—a couple.

Hotchner also felt they were narrowing in on the age of the UnSub. The last two kidnappings could have been done by a young person, except that even for a snatch job, these were pulled off with enough care that no one had seen the kidnapper. The abduction of Abigail Mathis was well thought out—had taken planning and nerve. The murders and disposals of the bodies were done with extreme care, as well.

Well organized, Hotchner thought again, *showing the patience of an older perpetrator.*

The pieces were coming together, but not fast enough. Getting ready to dig further, Hotchner looked up in surprise as Garue and JJ rushed in. The blonde agent was a pretty cool customer and her grave expression told Hotchner something major had gone down.

He asked, "What?"

"AMBER Alert," Garue said.

Morgan and Reid looked up from their work.

Jareau said, "A three-year-old blonde girl was just abducted from the back of her mother's SUV in Hibbing. Grabbed right out of her car seat in broad daylight."

Reid asked, "Where's Hibbing?"

Garue said, "Hundred ten miles east of here."

Morgan asked, "Is it our guy?"

"Only one way to find out," Hotchner said. "You and Garue get there now."

"On it," Morgan said, rose, and tossed on his jacket.

Turning to Jareau, Hotchner said, "Call Rossi and Prentiss and tell them the clock may be ticking even faster."

"Yes, sir."

"Reid, tell Garcia what's going on. Get her on this,

too. If this is our UnSub, we're closer than we've ever been. Let's move!"

Jesup, Georgia

Retired detective Malcolm Henry lived in a formidable two-story farmhouse just beyond the city limits on the far south side of town, a gravel lane leading up to the spread. Mickerson parked in front of a small but well-kept barn, and Rossi got out and looked around at something out of a Grant Wood painting.

A knock on a side door was answered by a short, thin woman in jeans and a gray sweatshirt with the words HILTON HEAD over the left breast. Seeing Mickerson made her smile and she invited them in.

They entered into a huge yellow kitchen dominated by an almost Arthurian-sized round oak dining table with matching chairs. Big windows on the south wall let in plenty of sunshine to make the room warm and inviting.

Mickerson asked, "How're you doing, Mrs. Henry?"

"Fine, fine," she said, with a wide smile. She was a petite woman who had stayed physically fit and appeared younger than the early sixties that Rossi figured her for, her hair color a shade of blonde unknown in nature.

After names had been exchanged and they'd all shaken hands, Mrs. Henry waved them to the table, saying, "Have a seat, have a seat. Would you like some coffee?"

Rossi said, "Sure, thanks."

Prentiss, Carlyle and Mickerson were game, as well.

When their hostess had given them all huge mugs of coffee, she said, "I expect you'll be wanting to talk to Mal."

"Yes, ma'am," Mickerson said. "Please."

She nodded. "I'll go and get him. He's—"

"He's right here," said a deep voice from the doorway off a dining room.

They all turned toward the basset-faced, barrel-chested, medium-sized man with the piercing brown eyes; his short dark hair was graying at the edges.

"Tim," Henry said as he strode in to join them. "How's my favorite bonus baby?"

"Bonus Baby's good, Mal. How's my favorite retiree?"

Henry gave up a single-shoulder shrug. "Gettin' by. This doesn't look like a social call. . . ."

Soon, the friendly Mrs. Henry having taken her leave, they were sitting together at the big table talking about the Abigail Mathis kidnapping.

"Figured it had to be that," Henry said with a husky sigh. "There are days when an old broke-down cop like me misses the job. But there aren't any days I miss *that* one."

Rossi asked, "What can you tell us?"

Henry sipped his coffee, then set the cup down.

"I'm glad somebody finally found the poor thing. I suppose you're after the perp now."

"Yeah. Who called and told you the girl had been identified?"

"Nobody," Henry said. "Made the local news—but there wasn't much in the way of details."

Rossi filled the retired detective in.

Henry chewed on the information awhile.

Rossi said, "The other girls buried with Abby could have been her sisters, they looked so much alike."

"That is plain goddamn weird."

"Yes, it is. But it's true—we've seen photos of each of the victims. They were all blonde girls abducted at age three or so, and killed between the ages of twelve and fourteen. All dressed nicely, all well taken care of."

"Took care of is right," Henry said gruffly. "All buried?"

"Next to each other," Rossi said. "The graves couldn't have been neater in a cemetery."

"All between twelve and fourteen, you say?"

"Yeah . . ."

Henry stroked his chin in thought, then turned to Mickerson. "When was that girl found in Bockman?"

"Oh, hell," Mickerson said, and grimaced. "Goddamn, I never even *thought* about that."

"What girl?" Prentiss asked.

The retired cop turned to her. "A blonde about the same age as your dead girls was found buried in the woods, outside Bockman."

Eyes flaring, she asked, "What and where is Bockman?"

"It's a town, sort of. Really only about seven or eight houses out the end of Sansavilla Road, on the south bank of the Altamaha River."

Rossi asked, "When was this?"

"Ten years ago," Henry said. "Never woulda even found her, but the river flooded that spring, and when the water went down, well, the grave was exposed. She was just sort of sticking up out of the ground. Wrapped in plastic like a goddamn sandwich."

Turning to Prentiss, Rossi asked, "How did we not get this information from Garcia?"

Henry held up a hand. "Ain't gonna be no record of this in VICAP, CASMIRC, or any of those kind of places."

The retired detective was referring to the FBI's Violent Criminal Apprehension Program and the Child Abduction and Serial Murder Investigations Resource Center.

Henry was saying, "Bockman is . . . rural. It ain't like here in town. They don't operate on any big scale. Hell, the sheriff thought he was lucky they called at all. Back there, in the woods, sometimes the dead get buried without a lot of . . . fanfare. 'You came from the earth, you shall return to the earth.' If the girl'd been from around there, they probably never would have called anyone. The mere fact that nobody recognized her, or her bracelet, was enough to get them to call the sheriff."

"Bracelet?" Prentiss asked.

"She was dressed nicely—I remember that from the photos I saw. Even though the water and the time in the ground had pretty much wrecked them, you could see the girl was wearing nice clothes. She also had a bracelet on her left wrist. Gold—sort of a really delicate ID bracelet, but instead of the girl's name, it had engraved in script 'Mommy's Little Sweetheart.'"

Rossi asked, "Was she ever identified?"

Frowning, Henry shook his head. "Nope. Sheriff called the Georgia Bureau of Investigation, and they did all they could, but the girl never got a name."

"Was there an autopsy?"

Henry shrugged. "I never heard of one. Being the county seat, we knew the sheriff and his department pretty well. That's how I found out as much as I did. Bockman's not anywhere near our jurisdiction. Once the state was involved, we sort of got shut out. The only thing I know for sure is the girl was never ID'd. You'd have to talk to the GBI to know for sure."

Rossi nodded. "We will. Hers was the only body found?"

"Far as I know."

"They didn't look for more graves?"

With a little shrug, Henry asked, "Why would they?"

Good point, Rossi thought.

They thanked their host for the time and information, and thanked Mrs. Henry, as well, who offered pie that they reluctantly turned down.

When they were out in the yard, Rossi turned to Mickerson. "How far is Bockman?"

"Maybe twenty miles."

"Is there somebody over there we could talk to? Somebody who would know where the body was found?"

"Sure, lots of folks."

Rossi frowned. "I mean *exactly* where."

Mickerson shrugged. "The sheriff would. He'd have been out there."

"Call him. Lead us out there, and we'll call the Georgia Bureau of Criminal Investigation on the way."

Mickerson asked, "What are you thinking?"

Rossi said, "I'm thinking I've just learned a blonde teenage girl was buried in the woods in Georgia. And I've learned this when I've come around investigating the deaths of blonde girls who disappeared from around here, ten years ago, who wound up buried in the woods of Minnesota."

"Doesn't sound like a coincidence."

"No. It doesn't. We need to see if there are more graves. There were three in Minnesota. Why would there only be *one* here? We have to look."

A call from JJ came in not long after they left Detective Henry's. Prentiss took it, then passed the message along to Rossi. A little blonde girl had been abducted from a town east of Bemidji and, Garcia said, Hotchner was afraid the whole cycle of kidnapping and murder might be starting again.

Prentiss asked, "Should we be back up there?"

"Our job is here," Rossi had said, matter-of-factly.

"The UnSub did his abductions on the road. He may have already left Bemidji."

Rossi nodded. "That's why we need to stay here. The more we find about the UnSub's past, the easier it'll be to predict his future."

"That makes sense," she admitted.

About Rossi's height and build, Sheriff Roger Okrent—an African-American in a black cowboy hat with the tan uniform of Wayne County—had short black hair, a black mustache, and brown eyes bright with intelligence. He was eager to help his FBI visitors.

Orkent led them to the spot in the woods—despite the lack of snow, a fair amount of green, and Georgia pines (not white-barked aspens), these cathedral-like, silently peaceful woods still much reminded Rossi of the Minnesota forest. But looking around the ground near where the girl had been found ten years ago, Rossi knew he might be standing near a hellish discovery.

Darkness settled into the Georgia woods before they could get the ground-penetrating radar down from Atlanta. That didn't stop Rossi. He found a company to rent them work lights and they illuminated the area like daylight.

The crime lab crew had worked the scene for four hours, midnight approaching, and Rossi was starting to wonder if he'd miscalculated. Prentiss wedged herself into the back of the SUV for a nap while Carlyle dozed in the driver's seat. Rossi stayed awake the whole time. He was thinking they would do one more grid, then call it a night.

"Hey!" the radar operator yelled. "I think we found something!"

Three hours of careful excavation later, the crime lab crew had opened two graves containing two plastic-wrapped skeletons that Rossi figured for teenage girls. They both wore dresses and both had wisps of blonde hair remaining.

Sheriff Okrent asked, "How the hell did you know they would be here?"

Rossi shook his head. "You have no idea how much I wish I'd been wrong. Tell me, who owns this forest?"

"Clenteen Industries," Okrent said. "Biggest lumber company in the area. Their office is in Brunswick."

"How far is that?"

"About thirty miles."

"We're going to need a motel in Brunswick," Rossi said. "The UnSub who killed these girls, and the three in Minnesota, worked there."

Chapter Eight

Bemidji, Minnesota

Derek Morgan had barely slept.

The trip to Hibbing had been both helpful and frustrating. Morgan and Garue had made the 105-mile drive in just over sixty minutes, Garue running the siren and pushing the gas pedal the whole way. They went directly to the police department on Twelfth Avenue E, were invited to join the investigation by Chief Nicole Barbaro, and then met with Detective Ian Hauser, a laconic, ruddy-faced, sad-eyed man who brought to mind a red-haired Abraham Lincoln.

Hauser filled them in on the information he had so far, which was scant. Even though the UnSub would have to have touched the SUV, the crime scene team had been unable to lift a single usable print that didn't belong to the Scheckel family. The only other hope was the store's security video.

After the catch-up meeting, Hauser joined Morgan and Garue for a ride to interview the missing child's parents, Thomas and Lisa Scheckel, at their log-cabin-style home on Lake Carey Road.

Mrs. Scheckel, Lisa—a blonde of twenty-five with even bangs, shoulder-length hair, and high, porcelain cheeks—wore an untucked pink button-down blouse with a wide belt at her jeans. Husband Thomas was a bearded bear of a man with brown hair as long as his wife's; his brown eyes burned in turns between rage and terror.

They sat in a living room whose log walls were home to leather furniture and a wall-mounted flat-screen TV above a glass shelving unit of electronic devices, with what were apparently mounted wireless surround-sound speakers. The Scheckels shared a sofa while Garue and Morgan sat in well-padded leather chairs at ninety-degree angles to the sofa. Detective Hauser stood at Garue's left shoulder.

After the introductions and Lisa's retelling the story of their daughter Sophie's disappearance, Morgan worked to get more details.

"Mr. Scheckel, what do you do for a living?"

"I'm an architect."

"For?"

Scheckel shook his head. "I guess you'd say I'm self-employed."

"Interesting work, architecture. Isn't this a prefab?"

"Yes. Which I designed for the company I co-own."

"Any trouble at work?" The profiler sat forward a little now.

"No. Not that I know of. My partners all seem happy."

"Clients?"

"I don't have anything to do with the clients who order our fabricated homes. And I haven't taken a private client on since we started the company."

Morgan gave the missing girl's mother a serious, supportive smile. "And, Mrs. Scheckel, do you work outside the home?"

She shrugged. "Just part-time at an independent bookstore."

"No trouble with relatives or friends?"

"This," Scheckel said tightly, "was a *stranger*—no one in our lives would do a thing like this."

Morgan kept his voice even. "We're just covering all the possibilities, sir. Mrs. Scheckel, have you noticed anyone suspicious hanging around your bookstore—following you, maybe?"

She frowned at that, thought for a moment, then shook her head.

Morgan turned to the husband. "Anything strange on your end, sir? Had the sense you were being followed in your car, maybe? A new face that's turned up where you take lunch, perhaps?"

"No. Everything in our life was just fine . . . until yesterday morning."

Morgan returned his attention to the mother. "Do you stop at that convenience store every day?"

"More like once or twice a week. Once a week anyway, for gas. They're the cheapest around here. Then, maybe once or twice more for a latte."

"Before or after you drop your daughter off?"

"Usually, when it's just coffee? After. But my gas

tank was in the red and I noticed the pumps were free, so I pulled in. Really just a spur-of-the-moment decision."

"So, do you stop for lattes the same days each week?"

"No. I don't think so anyway."

"Do you always take the same route to the day care?"

Mrs. Scheckel nodded. "Yes. There's really only one easy route, efficient route. Why?"

"I'm trying to establish if you have patterns someone watching you, over time, might ascertain. The individual we're tracking targets young girls who are of a type your daughter fits. That makes it less likely that an individual would have abducted your daughter on impulse."

Scheckel squeezed his wife's hand. "How much danger is Sophie in?"

"We do not believe she is in any immediate danger."

"Is this . . . is this a sexual predator?"

"Based upon the information we have, no. We believe this Unknown Subject takes children to essentially *adopt* and raise them."

Morgan did not add that, after a certain number of years, the girls would turn up murdered and buried in the woods.

Though he talked to the parents for another thirty minutes, Morgan learned nothing else new. That had been the frustrating part of the trip. The helpful part had been being able to send all the convenience store security video to Garcia. At least that held the possibility of a break.

Nothing else seemed to be working. The AMBER Alert that went out within thirty minutes of little Sophie's abduction had turned nothing up except that the usual cranks saw missing children the way other crazies saw UFOs.

Morgan already knew they were dealing with a ghost. Assuming this was their UnSub, he had kidnapped at least seven girls over the last twenty years, and not left so much as a fingerprint.

At the convenience store, Morgan studied the building, the parking lot, the gas pumps, everything about the place. Though the crime had gone down over four hours ago, the CSI van was still in the parking lot and traffic was crawling by as gawkers took it all in. Hauser went off to chat with the crime scene supervisor while Garue stayed with Morgan.

If Mrs. Scheckel had made such a spur-of-the-moment decision, how could the UnSub know the mother would be at the convenience store? The UnSub *must* have been following her. From where? Her house? The Scheckels lived out in the sticks.

The UnSub would be taking a hell of a risk parking anywhere near the house. Had he waited on a side road for them to pass, or had he waited in town somewhere? If she took the same route every day, the UnSub could easily wait anywhere along the route without being conspicuous.

If he knew the route, *how* did he know? How long had he been stalking this family?

"And why *this* family?" Morgan said aloud.

"What?" Garue asked.

"This family, the Scheckels. Why them?"

Garue shrugged. "Because they had a blonde, three-year-old daughter."

"Right—but how did he *know* that?"

Garue shrugged again.

"Because," Morgan said, "he had seen her. Where?"

The detective just stared this time, realizing he was not really part of the conversation.

"The day care," Morgan said. "That makes the most sense."

"What?" Garue asked.

"He staked out the day care. When he found the blonde child he liked, he followed when the mother picked her up."

"You sound sure of yourself."

Morgan gave the detective a curt nod. "I am. He staked them out, starting at the day care."

"For how long?"

With half a wry grin, Morgan said, "I'm a profiler, not a mystic. Now, let's figure out how he got the girl."

Morgan pointed out the cameras mounted on the roof, pointed toward the gas pumps—plain as the ass on a goat, like his old man used to say.

"The UnSub would have seen the security cams too," Morgan said to Garue, "and known not to park here. Cameras inside the store would catch the parking places near the front . . . difficult to tell, without going inside, whether they might catch other spots or not."

"Would our guy risk going inside to check?"

"Probably not. Going inside, he'd definitely get caught on camera, and this UnSub's just too careful for that."

"Grabbing a kid in broad daylight is careful?"

"In this instance, yes. Tell Detective Hauser to gather the security vids for the week preceding the abduction, just in case."

Garue went off and did that, and Morgan kept prowling the exterior of the store, thinking, thinking. . . .

If the UnSub didn't park on the property, where *had* he parked? For the UnSub to disappear so completely, so quickly, he couldn't have done this on foot, not on a street as busy as Twenty-fifth.

The UnSub had a vehicle.

A ghost vehicle, Morgan reminded himself. Something so bland and "normal" it would go unnoticed.

The side street west of the convenience store was less congested with traffic, but far from deserted. On the corner opposite was a gas station, with pumps on this side. Probably security cameras aimed this way, too, Morgan thought—another possibility to pass on to Detective Hauser, though Morgan figured the UnSub would likely have considered the same possibility.

As Morgan watched the gas station, his view was suddenly obstructed by a city bus that pulled up next to the convenience store, brakes whining, black exhaust affronting Morgan's nostrils. A bus stop on the corner—yet another reason not to park there; too much chance of a witness.

Morgan turned and saw, down the block, beyond the convenience store, a restaurant—a steak joint called Romano's. Nodding to himself, Morgan headed in that direction, along Twenty-fifth. The four-lane road had plenty of traffic. Crossing it, especially with a squirming, scared child, would be impossible without someone seeing the UnSub.

The restaurant was the only place that made sense.

The back of the restaurant faced the east side of the convenience store. As Morgan rounded the north side of the dark-wood-paneled exterior, he studied the perimeter of the building for any sort of security cameras. To his displeasure, he found nothing.

As he made his way around to the east side, Morgan saw a parking lot big enough for fifty cars. Was there a set of tire tracks here, belonging to the UnSub, taking off quickly with his prize?

The double glass doors into the restaurant were locked, the interior dark. The hours, listed on the glass, were four p.m. to eleven, and midnight Friday/Saturday.

Morgan went around front where the sign tried for elegance, ROMANO'S in red script, and below that, FOR THE BEST IN FINE DINING. Detracting from these upscale notions was a message board stating SATURDAY—ALL THE PRIME RIB YOU CAN EAT $19.99. Again, no cameras or security devices.

Hauser and Garue approached.

"Find anything?" the detective asked.

Morgan made his suggestion about the videos from the gas station across the street.

"Good idea," Hauser agreed. "Can we send those to your digital intelligence analyst, too?"

"You bet," Morgan said. "If there's anything there, she'll find it. You're going to want to lift tire prints from the parking lot of the restaurant next door."

"Why?"

"Because that's where he parked during the crime."

"How in hell can you know that?"

"It's what I do."

The Abe Lincoln look-alike frowned. "What makes you so sure?"

Morgan explained why that was the only place that made sense.

"Okay, Agent Morgan," Hauser said. "You sold me. I'll see that's done right away."

"Thank you."

Next they'd gone to the day care, where a series of interviews with the staff provided no help, and a short walk around the place revealed half a dozen vantage points from which the UnSub could have inconspicuously staked out the place. Morgan knew where Mrs. Scheckel had parked to pick up Sophie, and could narrow those hiding places down to about three; but could get no closer than that.

Thursday had been a long, hard day, and he and Garue had put in four more hours after they got back to Bemidji. The first had been spent briefing the team on what they'd found in Hibbing. The next three had

been spent responding to a neighbor's report that
Logan Tweed was back home, which finally allowed
an interview with the last hunter in the original discovery party.

When they had the lanky hunter in an interview
room, Garue and Morgan went in together. Per Morgan's instructions, the detective stayed mum after in-
troducing Morgan.

A skinny, hawk-nosed man with an unruly shock
of brown hair, Tweed wore jeans and a blue and
gray plaid flannel shirt over a white T-shirt.

Morgan got right to the point. "Where have you
been, Mr. Tweed?"

He shrugged. "I was on vacation. Everybody knew
I was going on vacation."

"Detective Garue, here, didn't. And hadn't Detective Garue told you to stay around? Didn't you know
it was inappropriate to leave town when you were
involved in a murder case?"

Tweed's eyes went to the detective, whose face
might have been cut from stone. "I wasn't *involved*!
I just came up, after Billy found the skeleton. Look,
I don't get a vacation every day. I was supposed to
go see my brother, so I went and saw my brother.
Sue me."

"This isn't really a civil matter, Mr. Tweed," Morgan said, unconvinced. "And where does your
brother live?"

Without hesitation, Tweed said, "Virginia."

"A deputy at a murder scene tells you to stay put,
and you travel halfway across the country?"

Looking confused, Tweed said, "Halfway where?"

Garue piped up. "Agent Morgan, Virginia is a town about two hours east of here."

Morgan nodded sourly.

Tweed looked pleased with himself.

Eyes unblinking, Garue said to Morgan, "It's on the other side of Hibbing."

Now it was Morgan's turn to smile and Tweed's to look uncomfortable.

Tweed said, "So it's on the other side of Hibbing—so what?"

Morgan ignored that. "When did you get back from Virginia?"

With a little shrug, Tweed said, "Late last night."

"Tell me about it."

"I drove home, got the message you guys left on my machine, and was going to come in tomorrow, if my neighbors hadn't got nosy." He shrugged. "That's pretty much it."

Morgan asked, "What route did you take on your return?"

"One Sixty-nine to Grand Rapids, then Highway Two home. Why?"

Ignoring that as well, Morgan asked, "So that took you through Hibbing?"

"Yeah, I guess, sure—I drive that route all the time."

"Interesting," Morgan said. "Would you happen to know what went down in Hibbing yesterday?"

"No. What?"

"A little blonde girl was kidnapped," Morgan said,

his voice hard and cold. "Victim the same age and general appearances as the girls you found, when they were abducted."

"Those . . . those were grown girls, weren't they?"

"Little girls when they were abducted, Mr. Tweed. Grown girls when they were murdered."

Tweed sat there for maybe thirty seconds, saying nothing, as Morgan just stared at him, the way a snake regards a bug.

Finally, the hawk-nosed man looked up. "You can't think *I* had something to do with this?"

Morgan said, "You're pals with Rohl, aren't you?"

"Who?"

"Kwitcher, Billy Kwitcher. You didn't know his real name was Rohl? And that he's a sex offender from Arkansas?"

"*That* twerp?" Tweed held his hands up in surrender. "I had no damn *idea!*"

"You boys both fit the profile we've been developing about this killer."

Tweed had a clubbed-baby-seal expression.

"Was the burial site part of the plan," Morgan pressed, "so you two could gaze across your conquests while you were hunting? And revel in your shared secret?"

Aghast, Tweed said, "No! No goddamn way! I never knew that side of Billy—to me he was just this sad-sack loser, and I sure as hell ain't into kiddie porn. I don't want any part of that shit, or any part of *Billy*, neither."

Morgan studied the man. Either he was telling the

truth or Logan Tweed was a world-class liar. Still, Rohl/Kwitcher had lived within driving distance of the original abductions, and even though Billy had done time in Arkansas, that didn't preclude Tweed from somehow having had custody of the girls before they all moved up here.

Morgan asked, "When did you meet Billy Rohl?"

"Billy Kwitcher, you mean? Not long after he moved up here, I guess. Late 2005, maybe?"

"Are you asking me or telling me?"

"I'm *telling* you. . . . Do I need a lawyer?"

"Do you?"

"I'm not answering another question without a lawyer!"

With a dismissive shrug, Morgan said, "You can go."

Tweed reared back, startled. Then he jumped to his feet and made a beeline for the exit.

When Tweed's hand had just grasped the doorknob, Morgan said, "There is one more thing, Mr. Tweed."

Tweed looked petrified to have come so close to freedom and then be stopped. He turned toward Morgan, ashen. "What?"

"Stay close. We might want to talk to you again."

"Sure," Tweed said. "Understood."

Morgan's voice was sharp. " 'Stay close' means in town. Not at your brother's. Not in Mexico. Not in Canada. If we have to hunt you down, Mr. Tweed— you have my personal guarantee it will not be pleasant."

Tweed swallowed, nodded, and ducked out.

Garue, frowning, asked, "Is there a reason you're letting him go?"

"Let's start with, we've got nothing to hold him on. Anyway, when we first arrived, you told us that he and Dan Abner were lifelong residents, right?"

"Right."

"Well," Morgan said, "unless we can tie Tweed to Rohl prior to 'oh five, we can't tie him to the original three abductions. He could have helped with the homicides, but neither Billy nor Logan seems to have the dominant personality it'd take to kill those girls."

"So you think he's innocent?"

"I do," Morgan admitted. "That's got nothing to do with it, though—we'll get Garcia to find a connection if there is one, but I'd be surprised if Tweed knew Rohl before 2005."

With the Tweed interview under his belt, Morgan still had three more waiting—the foresters from Bassinko Industries: Lawrence Silvan, Randy Beck, and Jason Fryman.

The trio sat in chairs lining the hall outside the conference room. Before Morgan could ask which wanted to go first, Reid stuck his head out the door.

"Better get in here," Reid said. "Rossi's online with some information that Hotchner wants us all to hear."

Morgan shut the conference room door behind him. JJ was at her laptop with Reid and Hotchner peering over her shoulders. When he joined them to look at the screen, Rossi—courtesy of Garcia, no doubt—was waiting.

"Okay," Hotchner said. "We're all here, Dave—what have you got?"

"Three more dead girls," Rossi said. "Same UnSub—he killed three down here before moving to Minnesota."

Hotchner asked, "Do we know where these girls are from?"

"Garcia's working on that now, along with the Georgia Bureau of Criminal Investigation."

"Details?"

"Three teenage girls buried next to each other just as in Bemidji."

Reid said, "It's not like blonde girls buried in threes is something that comes up regularly—how did we not know about them?"

Rossi explained how only one death had been known about, and how he and Prentiss had led the team that unearthed the other two.

"Dave," Hotchner said, clearly impressed, "good work."

"The land the bodies were buried in," Rossi said, "is owned by Clenteen Industries—a lumber company."

Reid and Morgan traded glances at this significant news, but Hotchner didn't even have to think about it.

"Let's get Garcia going," the team leader said, "on tracking employees who left Clenteen Industries, and went to work for Bassinko over the last ten years."

Garcia popped up, her smaller image next to Rossi's, as she did her magic with conference video.

She said perkily, "Already have the list, sir."

Hotchner asked, "How many names on it?"

"Seven."

"That seems high."

"Clenteen and Basinko are both owned by a huge holding company, the MRST Corporation. This allows employees who might be laid off at one plant to transfer to another, depending on where needed and, of course, seniority. Over the same period, six employees went in the other direction."

Morgan said, "We need to narrow the list."

Garcia said, "Three of the seven moved up there within the last year."

Rossi said, "If I'm right, and the UnSub made a run for it ten years ago, we can eliminate those three. I think the flood causing the first body to be found was the stressor that forced the UnSub to run."

Hotchner said, "In that case, we only need the transfers that happened ten years ago. . . . Garcia, how many of the employees transferred ten years ago?"

Garcia rolled out of view to check another screen, then rolled back. "Two—Lawrence Silvan and Jason Fryman."

"Let's concentrate on them," Hotchner said. "Rossi, you and Prentiss keep working with Garcia to identify the bodies of the Georgia victims."

"Already on it," Rossi said.

His image disappeared, and then so did Garcia's. Hotchner passed out instructions to Reid and JJ, who were charged with putting the final pieces of the profile together, to brief the local police once Morgan was finished.

"Morgan," Hotchner said, "interview all three foresters."

"Not just Silvan and Fryman?"

Beck was a burly guy, easily capable of carrying any of the victims halfway across Minnesota. He would not have had to bury the girls that close to the road. A lifelong Bemidji resident who'd worked for Bassinko for twenty years, he couldn't fit into the profile with a shoehorn.

"No," Hotchner said. "Use Beck as a sort of control, to try to gain insight into the other two."

"Got ya."

Randy Beck—a hulk of fifty with a blond brush cut going to gray, in jeans, a blue work shirt, and boots—seemed to fill the corridor as they walked to the interview room.

When they were seated, Morgan led the forester through some preliminary background questions. Married, with two kids, Beck had gotten a summer job with Bassinko right out of high school and worked there every summer through college. Once he graduated, he started working his way up.

Morgan said, "Tell me about your job."

"Inspecting new growth, mostly," Beck said. "We go to different forests across Minnesota, all owned by Bassinko, and we count new stems, take soil samples, measure the new growth, that sort of thing."

"Do you have designated areas?"

Beck shrugged. "We get grids from the office, and those are the areas we work."

"So—any of you could end up in forest four?"

"Yeah, I guess, but we tend to stay with places we already worked. So, sort of by default, it winds up being kind of territorial."

"Which of you spends the most time in forest four?"

Another shrug. "All of us do—it's eighty acres and there's plenty of work. That one's an exception. It's also the closest to home. The other forests, those we sort of divvy up on our own."

"Divided how?"

"I work the south, Cass County, mostly. Silvan has the area north, around Blackduck? And Fryman, he has the eastern territory, around Grand Rapids."

"And whose territory would include Hibbing?"

"That's east. Fryman."

"Thank you, sir."

Beck left and was replaced in the interview room by Lawrence Silvan. The bespectacled forester seemed out of place in jeans, work boots, and long-sleeved work shirt with BASSINKO over the left breast.

Morgan asked Silvan the same questions as Beck and received largely the same answers.

Morgan asked, "Are you married?"

"Yeah," Silvan said, his look slightly quizzical over the sudden turn in the conversation.

"Were you married when you moved up here from Georgia?"

Silvan studied Morgan for a long moment. "How did you know I moved here from Georgia?"

"Routine background check on Bassinko employees from the list you gave us. Were you married when you moved up here?"

"Yeah," Silvan said. "College sweethearts. Why is that important?"

"We're asking certain questions of everyone involved," Morgan said vaguely. "For profiling purposes. Why did you leave Georgia?"

"I got the chance to make more money. Better opportunity than staying in Brunswick."

Theories abounded on how to tell if a person was lying. Profilers like Morgan built up pretty good bullshit detectors, but he'd had people lie right to his face and still had no idea. Sociopaths were masters at this.

"We liked Georgia," Silvan was saying. "Weather was great, and of course up here it's colder than a witch's you-know-what in winter. But, still, there's been far more opportunity in Bemidji."

"Did you know Jason Fryman in Brunswick?"

Nodding, Silvan said, "Sure, Jason and I've been going after the same jobs at the same time our whole career. He graduated from Kent State same time I came out of Iowa State. Both started at Clenteen, same time. When MRST bought Clenteen and Bassinko, that made more opportunities for a lot of people. Some took early retirement, and that made openings for Jason and me, up here."

"You two close?"

Silvan shrugged. "Not really. More like friendly acquaintances."

"What do you know about his family life?"

"Not much."

"What *do* you know, Mr. Silvan?"

"Well, he's married."

"Kids?"

"Not that I know of."

"How about you?"

"Kids aren't really for us," Silvan said. "Between my job and my wife's career, well, there's just never been time."

"What does your wife do?"

"She works out of the house. She's a teacher."

"How is it a teacher works out of the house?"

"She works with homeschoolers."

Morgan talked to Silvan a while longer, for all the good it did.

Blond, sallow-faced, with sad blue eyes, Jason Fryman looked like he'd been the skinny kid who regularly got his ass kicked by the school bully. In his early forties, Fryman wore the same uniform as the others—blue work shirt with company crest, jeans, and boots—and yet even the smaller Silvan had seemed more imposing than Fryman.

As he had with the other two, Morgan went through the questions about their jobs. Fryman's answers were pretty much what Morgan had already heard.

"Married?" Morgan asked.

Fryman nodded. "You?"

Morgan smiled. "Haven't found the right one yet."

"You will," Fryman said. He smiled, too. "Nothing like it."

"So I've heard. How long?"

"Twenty-two wonderful years."

"You got kids?"

Fryman's smile faded. "No. My wife miscarried with what would have been our first, twenty years ago. There were . . . complications."

"Sorry."

Fryman shrugged. "Life isn't easy for anybody, is it?"

"Not really. Why did you leave Georgia?"

The forester mulled that, eyes on the table, fingers busy worrying the button on a ballpoint pen. "Too many bad memories, I guess. That was where Amy lost the baby. We just had to get out of there. When the opportunity came, to come up here? Why, I jumped on it."

"And your marriage survived all of that?"

"Don't get me wrong. We had our ups and downs."

"Did you ever think about adoption?"

Fryman clicked the ballpoint even faster now, caught himself, looked down at the pen and managed to let it drop on the table. "My wife has always been . . . particular."

Morgan wondered if he was about to hear a confession. This wouldn't be the first time that an UnSub confessed at the first hint of pressure. Instead of exerting more, Morgan decided to let Fryman pressure himself.

"When Amy found out we couldn't adopt just the right child"—the little man shrugged—"that was the end of that."

Morgan waited for the other shoe to drop.

Picking up the pen, its pull too much for him, Fryman clicked the ballpoint. "So . . . we've never had children."

Morgan decided to try a nudge. "Hibbing's in your territory, isn't it?"

"Yeah."

"You hear about what happened there yesterday?"

Looking up, still clicking away, Fryman said, "It was on the news. Terrible, terrible thing."

"Were you in Hibbing yesterday?"

Fryman shook his head. "I called in sick yesterday. Larry covered for me."

"Was *he* in Hibbing yesterday?"

"You'll have to ask Larry."

Morgan, arching an eyebrow, said, "You didn't exactly jump to his defense to say he couldn't have done it."

"Why, would you have taken my word for it?"

Allowing himself a small smile, Morgan said, "No, no, I wouldn't."

"That's what I thought. So why waste my breath telling you that neither one of us would do something terrible like that?"

"You understand, we have to look into the possibility where both of you are concerned."

Rising, Fryman said with understated but nonetheless surprising defiance, "Look away. Do whatever you want. You'll be wasting your time, though. Somewhere out there's a kidnapper . . . and instead of looking for him, you're going to be wasting your time looking into Larry and me. A couple of good, upstanding citizens. Is that how the three girls here fell through the cracks?''

As Fryman strode out of the room, Morgan could only wonder if he had just been taunted by a serial killer.

Chapter Nine

Brunswick, Georgia

Life spent continually on the road, without a bag big enough to check at the airport, made packing for a long trip a challenge that rivaled finding something healthy to eat in a break-room vending machine. Anyone who thought the lives of the BAU team were glamorous—thanks to high-profile cases and the hero-making best sellers by Max Ryan, John Douglas and David Rossi himself, among others—were sadly misinformed.

The BAU members might be away from home for as much as a month at a time. They had to find Laundromats, places to eat that weren't simply fast food (though there was plenty of that), and lodging within the bureau's less than generous budget, to accompany the long hours spent in police stations or field offices around the country.

A saving grace of this trip had been the excellent laundry facilities inside the hotel in Bemidji. Since then, however, an itinerary of Minnesota to Georgia to Alabama, and presumably back again, had given Emily Prentiss no chance to do her laundry.

And with the all-nighter at the grave sites last night, Prentiss hadn't even had time to change her clothes or brush her teeth. Thankfully, a breath strip and her pocket hand sanitizer kept her from feeling terminally gross.

Rossi had planned to get them checked into a motel to clean up and catch a quick nap, but events had conspired against them.

First, they'd attended hastily scheduled autopsies of the two new bodies the crime lab team had unearthed. The smell had been minimal compared to an ordinary autopsy, the bodies having been buried for so long that the soft tissue was gone, and the aroma with it.

Some things had survived the prolonged interment, including tufts of the girls' blonde hair; also present were shreds of clothing. Like the three girls in Minnesota, these victims had been buried in nice clothes, wrapped in blankets and sheets of plastic— much of the plastic and some of the blankets had survived as well.

The clothes, like those in Minnesota, had no tags and appeared homemade. The most surprising discovery was a little pink purse, inside of which were a stubby pencil, a comb, and a tampon still in its plastic applicator.

Rossi held up the plastic evidence bag containing the tampon. "Half the girls had these and the other half were of an age when they'd be getting their first period. Significant?"

Prentiss frowned in thought and nodded. "I think it might be. . . ."

"Me, too," Rossi said. "Me, too . . ."

Cohasset, Minnesota

Things were moving fast now. Possibly too fast. Though he had expected the FBI to talk to him at some point, he was surprised by how much they already knew. Normally, he never would have shopped two days in a row, but these were not normal conditions.

In less than two days, he and His Beloved would be on the road. He would have preferred to let things settle more before they left, but those darn hunters had disrupted his timetable. Even worse, they'd disturbed the peaceful resting place he'd bestowed their girls. One of the hunters was still being held by the cops, but the *other* two . . .

How he would love to punish them for what they had done—killing was too good for them, but it would have sufficed. For now he would have to be content with daydreams of torturing them, making them pay for upsetting his life, his family—this, at least, gave him a modicum of pleasure as he drove to Cohasset, a little town northwest of Grand Rapids.

Though the drive was only sixty-five miles down U.S. 2, he had taken the long way around, going south on U.S. 71 to Minnesota 200, then east through Whipholt and Remer before turning north to Cohasset. He took the roundabout route to be seen working, away from the town where he would adopt another girl. He had been in the little town before, and done some window-shopping there, just in case.

His methodical planning, always a major priority for him, had come in especially handy this time. If he hadn't already had his eye on a little girl in Cohasset, they wouldn't be able to build their family in nearly enough time. That was the nice thing about his job—it gave him a certain freedom, to keep his eyes open for possibilities.

Wasn't like he hadn't known what was coming. He had tried to talk His Beloved out of sending the girls to finishing school, but their future was out of his hands. No matter how much he pleaded with her, he never had a chance. Neither did their girls. He had known this, especially after the first time.

The little girl in Cohasset was special. He did not want to let this one get away. Besides, after Hibbing, the authorities were all looking to the east. Having a second abduction so quickly, so close to the other, would keep their attention to the east while he, His Beloved, and their new family would head west toward Washington State, and a new life.

He had gotten a job with a lumber company near Seattle, but had explained to them that he would not be able to start until after the first of the year.

That meant nearly two months with no income, but they had been saving for quite a while, and were prepared to lie low for the next month or so. Plus, once he had become aware the federals were on the way, he'd immediately asked to use two weeks of vacation he'd been saving, for just such an emergency. He would give them his resignation soon enough, but he was in no hurry. No point in giving the federals a leg up.

As he drove down the tree-lined two-lane, the aspens cast soothing shadows across the road. Once again, he reconsidered his plan to shift the blame. Even back in Georgia a plan had been in place— had the police picked up his trail too soon, he would've fed them someone he'd lined up to take his fall. The same was true now. Almost since their arrival in Bemidji, he had been scouting for someone to take the heat, should things play out that way.

The plan was set and, after today, he would probably have to make sure that information about the individual he'd chosen began to find its way into the hands of the FBI. Otherwise, no amount of lying low would allow their family to surface using their real name. That would mean giving up his job, his degree, and sacrificing all the years he'd put into the lumber industry.

Of course, if necessary, he would start again under a new name. After all, everything else was secondary to keeping His Beloved happy and safe; but for the last twenty-five years, he had been able to protect her and hold on to his career.

That was a long time to work so hard, but he was

proud of what he and His Beloved had built up over the years. Yes, finishing school *had* deprived him of watching the girls fully mature, but they were a blessing for the time they were in his life. And considering this corrupt and immoral world, the girls were lucky to have the lifetimes they'd enjoyed, however truncated.

If the frame he'd constructed was as tight as he thought, his foil would take the blame for everything that had happened here, and perhaps the events in Georgia as well.

He entered the town and eased down the main street. Cohasset was too small to have a police department—a plus for him. With a population of 2,500, their protection came from the Itasca County Sheriff's Office. Today, after the word went out, the police departments of Coleraine, Grand Rapids, Hill City and Deer River would all be involved as well. He knew that. He also knew that by the time they started blocking roads, he'd be long gone— and so would the girl.

He made sure none of the deputies' cars were in front of the diner. In a town with no police, he'd feel humiliated after planning this shopping trip so carefully, only to have it go to h-e-double-l because some deputy was having lunch two blocks from his target.

Luckily, the diner, though busy, showed no signs of law enforcement. He traveled southeast on U.S. 2 past the diner, before turning left on Columbus

Avenue, then circling the block back to the highway.

He crossed the highway to the southwest on First Avenue NW and rolled over the Burlington Northern Santa Fe rail crossing—the only thing that could disrupt his plan. Three routes of exit from the neighborhood he was entering would take him back to U.S. 2. He could come back the way he came, or use two other outlets to the north. The only downside was that all three crossed the railroad tracks at some point.

One off-schedule freight train, and he would be boxed in.

He had checked the train schedule carefully and found a train due through here just after one, but that still gave him over an hour. You heard about trains being late, but never about them running early! That better hold up today. The only other way out was a four-mile sprint dead west on a two-lane county road. If the police got in front of him, it would all be over.

The house he was looking for was on Fourth Avenue, a north-south street with only four residences on the west side between First and Second streets. The third house on the left, a white clapboard bungalow, was the home of the little blonde girl he had his eye on.

He had seen her for the first time in the diner back on the highway. After stopping there for lunch one afternoon (in the summer when he had been working in the area), he became mesmerized by the little girl when she came in with her mother. As they ate, he had watched them, and dawdled over several cups of coffee after he'd finished his lunch, then followed them out when they left. The woman had loaded the child into a car seat in the back of a blue Ford Focus. He memorized the license number just in case he lost them. Wasn't like it was that big a town. . . .

He spent another half hour following the Focus to a gas station, then to the post office, before the woman had finally driven home. Two more trips over the end of summer and into the fall had determined that the Focus was always parked in the gravel driveway. As he eased past the house, he noted the Focus in the driveway—Mommy was home, presumably, which meant the girl would be there, too.

In a town this small, he did not dare park; the chance of somebody noticing his car was too great. Again, as he had in Hibbing, he'd rented a car. This Ford Taurus was unassuming and looked as if it might belong to the insurance salesman he pretended to be. To cover his tracks further, he had stopped at a roadside restaurant for breakfast.

He'd chosen the restaurant because the parking lot had another Taurus—a different color than his rental, but that didn't matter. The subterfuge didn't have to hold up for long; it just had to buy him a few more minutes. Any edge, however small, was a good edge.

Since he had neither the skills nor the nerve to steal a car, he did the next best thing: He parked next to the other Taurus, and—under the pretext of tying his shoe—knelt behind the vehicle and, his heart pounding, got out a small screwdriver.

Working quickly and cautiously, he removed the rear license plate, tucked it under his Windbreaker, then rose, returned to his car, tossed the plate into the trunk, and shut it. He hoped the other Taurus would pull out of the lot with its driver not missing his rear plate—and even if the plate's absence *was* noticed, the driver would hardly heed the car next to him—he'd simply think that vandals had swiped the plate or, perhaps, that the bumpy Minnesota two-lane roads had knocked it off.

Walking to the restaurant, he struggled to get his breathing under control. He even stopped and bought a *USA Today* out of the machine and took three deep breaths as he took one more look around the lot to make sure his petty theft had gone unnoticed. He realized he was breaking his own rule of never committing a misdemeanor while committing a felony, but he had not, as of yet, committed that felony. So, he thought, the argument at this point was purely academic.

That thought gave him a smile as he entered the restaurant and had a hearty breakfast. He even left the waitress a better-than-usual tip, so she would remember him—he had still been wearing his company shirt and jeans under the company Windbreaker. After breakfast, he drove to one of his inspection points. He performed the inspection, then, with the rental car parked well off the road, changed into his suit and switched the rear license plate for the one from the diner.

Now, an hour later, feeling he'd covered his tracks, he made one more pass through the neighborhood, pretending to be looking for a house number, but really checking out the block for walkers and anyone stepping out onto their porches. From his vantage point, the neighborhood looked quieter than the forests he knew so well.

He turned into the driveway, took a deep breath to try to settle his grinding stomach, then checked his disguise in the rearview mirror. The fake mustache and cheap black wig weren't terribly believable up close, but from a distance should work. Next, he slipped on a pair of latex gloves. He wasn't in any fingerprint database that he was aware of, never having been arrested or served in the military, but taking chances was ill-advised.

He stepped from the car with a black shoulder bag that he hoped would make his insurance man disguise more believable, should any neighbors spot him. More importantly, he had the top flap open and one hand stuck inside. There was only one chance here, and the prize was breathtaking.

He had to get it right.

He climbed the two concrete steps to the door, and rang the bell. A screen door separated him from the locked inner door, half wood, half glass with curtains. Through the divide, he could see the blonde woman coming to the door. She seemed perplexed by this interruption in her day. Her eyes cut down the hallway toward what he presumed was a bedroom, and he hoped that the little girl was taking a midday nap. That might make his job easier.

When the woman's eyes fell on him, he smiled. Though the confusion didn't completely leave her face, the small-town girl smiled—pretty, almost as tall as him, slim with her blonde hair tied back today. She wore faded jeans and a maroon University of Minnesota sweatshirt with gold lettering and Goldy, the team mascot, on it.

She unlocked the dead bolt, opened the inner door, and, in what was a very helpful move to him, opened the screen.

Her smile was wide if still uncomprehending. "May I help—"

That was as far as she got before his hand came out of the shoulder bag with the Taser clutched in his fist.

He fired the weapon and the tiny darts struck her in the chest. The woman's eyes widened almost comically and her mouth formed a soundless O as she jumped and jerked, falling backward into the house.

He glanced around, saw no one on the street or on the porches of the nearby houses, and simply followed the still-shuddering woman inside. She fell to the hardwood floor of the living room, the wires between them dancing as she convulsed. He looked around at the room—tastefully decorated with a brown cloth-covered sofa, love seat and wide chair with hassock. A squat rectangular table sat in the middle of the grouping, the little girl's toys cluttering the floor.

He closed the door, looking through the window once more to make sure the coast was clear. Looking down, he noted the woman had passed out. He bent to her and pulled the darts out of the Minnesota sweatshirt—most of Goldy the Gopher's face had been obliterated and droplets of blood were left behind on the maroon sweatshirt.

He withdrew a small bottle of chloroform from the bag, along with a rag, undid the cap (careful to keep it at arm's length) and poured a little onto the cloth. To make sure he had time to accomplish his goal, he held the thing to the woman's nose for a count of ten.

She was definitely going to be out for a while.

He hoped she wouldn't remember anything about him, but if she did, she'd be hard-pressed to come up with anything beyond his disguise.

As he turned toward the hallway to the bedrooms, he saw the small blonde girl staring up at him, her expression perplexed.

"What did you do to my mommy?" she asked.

"She was tired," he said gently, his voice low and even, despite his surprise at seeing the little girl. "Now she's taking a nap."

Her cornsilk hair framed a heart-shaped face; she had a glowing porcelain complexion. Her blue eyes were the color of the sky on a sunny day, even as they filled with tears and she ran to her fallen mother.

But she did not wail or scream, nor did she run away from him. Instead, she knelt at her mother's side as if to say good-bye. It was almost as if she'd chosen to go with him, which warmed his heart as he scooped her up and put the cloth over her mouth.

She struggled for only a moment.

He rested the quiet child on the floor, using her mother's arms as a pillow. The little girl was so beautiful—he felt a tear roll down his cheek. This gift would make His Beloved so happy.

A thrill came from being inside this foreign house. He had only been in one other such house—that of Ellen, their first, with her parents sleeping in the next room. All he had been able to do then was collect his precious gift and run.

Today, he could shop for accessories.

The first thing he did was tie up the mother and gag her. Fifteen minutes later, he'd packed a small bag of toys and clothes, which he ran outside with and put in the trunk, leaving the lid up. The neighborhood remained quiet and he rushed back inside to gather his blanket-wrapped prize. Carrying her down the two steps and across the yard, his heart pounding, he slowly scanned every house across the street, watching for anyone who might see him.

Nothing. No one.

After placing her carefully in the trunk, he closed the lid and once again looked around before he

climbed into the car and, as calmly as he could,
backed out of the driveway and headed for his own
vehicle. He hated having to put the precious child
in the trunk, and was anxious to get her safely into
her waiting car seat.

Bemidji, Minnesota

Dr. Spencer Reid ached from head to toe.

The youngest of the BAU team felt one hundred
years old. The lack of sleep, from working nearly
twenty-hour days with no breaks, had worn him out,
both physically and mentally. He had a pounding
tension headache and wanted nothing more than to
close his eyes for an hour or two.

What kept him going was knowing that Hotchner,
Morgan, and Jareau felt at least as drained. In the
five days they'd been here, they had made significant
progress; but they'd sent two members of the team
to Georgia, making more work for those left behind.
Even Detective Garue, who'd been with them every
day, looked like he'd been on a weeklong stakeout.

The video feed on his laptop came alive and Reid
found himself staring not at Garcia, but at David
Rossi.

"Hotch there?" Rossi asked.

Hotchner stepped over to Reid's laptop, Morgan
on his heels. "You have something, Dave?"

Rossi held up the evidence bag with the purse in
it. "This belonged to one of the girls," he said. "She
was buried with it."

"And?"

"And inside, there was a tampon."

They all stared blankly at the laptop for a long second as if they had heard Rossi wrong.

Reid got it in an intuitive flash. "He loves them as girls, but he can't tolerate them as women. That's why he kills them—they're turning into women."

Eyes flaring, Morgan said, "That goes along with our theory that he's an incomplete personality—that he can't maintain a normal relationship."

"Also speaks to his control issues," Hotchner said. "Once they start menstruating, they've moved beyond his control, at least in his mind, and he can't stand it."

Reid blurted, "But we've been working as if this UnSub is a pedophile."

In the room, Morgan and Hotchner stared at him, and from the laptop, Rossi did the same.

"I'm just saying," Reid went on, "pedophiles have very narrow interests. This UnSub has been holding these girls for long periods of time, much longer than a normal pedophile would."

"True," Rossi said, frowning from the laptop. "I think Reid might be onto something. This problem might be more complicated than simple pedophilia."

"All right," Morgan said. "So—where does that leave us?"

For several moments no one said anything, as they all reconsidered their information so far.

"Has to be a couple," Reid said, as if to himself.

"What?" Hotchner asked.

"A *couple*," Reid said. "A childless couple who wanted children, girls specifically, but for some reason, after they reach puberty, they become, what, obsolete? Or dangerous?"

"Or," Rossi said from the screen, "they become competition."

Morgan's eyes tightened. "Competition how?"

"Not 'how'—*who*," Rossi said. "For the mother. She sees them as her competition with the father . . . *sexually*, once they reach puberty."

"Acting out," Hotchner said, "from abuse she probably received herself as a young woman."

"Probably," Rossi said, "from her father."

Hotchner twitched a frown. "Are we sure this is the right direction?"

Rossi said, "Makes sense to me. First time the pieces have seemed to fit."

Garue asked, "Could a woman like that have anything like a normal relationship with a man?"

"If she did," Reid said, eyes slits, "wouldn't the characteristics of that man be nonthreatening? Insufficient personality? Avoids confrontation? Despises violence? And aren't these the characteristics we've already applied to our UnSub?"

They were all staring at him now, and if he'd been forced to answer, Reid would admit that he enjoyed the respect he saw in their eyes.

"Let's get the locals in," Hotchner said. "Let's not waste any more time—let's give them the profile."

The detectives, deputies, and city patrolmen who crowded into the conference room that had served as the team's home for this week were loud as they chattered among themselves. Hotchner, Morgan, and Reid stood up front with Detective Garue. JJ was off dealing with the media, trying to keep the story from blowing up nationally on the cable news outlets—in the long run, they all knew, that would be a vain attempt.

Stepping forward, Hotchner cleared his throat and the cops straightened up and quieted down. "I'm sure by now you've all heard that this case is not just a local one. This UnSub has killed at least six girls in two states over the last ten years, and abducted them over an even longer period."

The surprised officers glanced at each other, some shook their heads, some mumbled epithets.

Again Hotchner waited for quiet, then said, "The media will try to play this case up as a sex crime and the UnSub as a pedophile."

Some cops nodded. The rumors had already started.

"We don't believe this to be the case."

They looked at him skeptically.

A uniform asked, "How is this guy not some kind of perv?"

The profilers all winced at the word choice, but no one said anything—they were guests here. Hotchner turned to Reid, who explained about pedophiles, and how these girls had been held much longer than was typical.

When Reid finished, a detective asked, "Then what the hell *is* going on here?"

Hotchner said, "Kidnappings happen for three reasons: profit, perversity, and to gain a child. No victims' parents ever received a ransom note here, so profit was not the motive. We believe, as we've already explained, that sexual abuse was also not the motive. That leaves only one—to replace or gain a child."

The skepticism in the officers' faces faded a little.

"We think we're looking for a married, or at least long-term, couple. He will be nonconfrontational and believe himself to be less than most men. Physically, he will not be imposing and will have trouble maintaining eye contact, especially with figures of authority. We believe he works for Bassinko Industries. We have, in fact, narrowed the field of suspects to four. Two of them moved well after the crimes in Georgia. We'll have some of you go interview them just to be sure. The other two suspects, Jason Fryman and Lawrence Silvan, both fit the profile in most every aspect. Both are married and childless, both left Georgia within one month of the discovery of the first body there."

The officers were all taking notes now and Morgan was passing out photos of the two main suspects.

"As for the wife of the UnSub, she is probably a victim of child abuse, and may well be the dominant partner. We expect she is the one committing the murders while the more submissive partner—the husband—abducts the victims, then, when the time has come, disposes of the bodies."

The officers were all attentive now.

"Another thing," Morgan said, getting to the back

of the room and forcing the policemen to turn their heads. "Just because we've painted this male UnSub as Casper P. Milquetoast, don't for a second believe he's not dangerous. If he thinks we're threatening his family, or his dominant partner, he will fight to protect them. He will *kill* to protect them. So don't be deceived."

"That's right," Hotchner said. "And—"

He was interrupted by a knock at the conference room door. Before he could stop her, a Bemidji police dispatcher burst into the room. "There's been another abduction! The AMBER Alert just came out."

"Where?" Hotchner asked.

"Itasca County. Cohasset."

Reid swung toward Detective Garue.

"East of here," Garue said, "near Grand Rapids."

"Let's get to it," Hotchner said over the sudden din of chatter and squeaking chairs as they were pushed back and the officers rose. "Get your assignments from your superiors."

The officers rushed out, as Morgan came over to join Reid, Garue, and Hotchner.

Hotchner said, "Let's find Fryman and Silvan now."

Morgan shook his head, growling, "Damnit, I knew we should have tailed them."

Shrugging, Hotchner said, "That was my call. I thought it was premature."

"Well, it wasn't." Then Morgan seemed embarrassed. "Sorry, Hotch. . . ."

"No, you're right. But even now we don't have

enough agents to do it, and these locals don't have the experience to not be made. Someone had to make the decision. I'll carry the weight of it."

Reid had never been jealous of command, and even less so now. As he studied Hotchner, his boss seemed to be aging before his eyes. The stress level of their job, always high, had just tripled. A second child abducted within twenty-four hours.

But enough of self-recrimination.

Time for the BAU team to earn their paychecks.

Chapter Ten

Brunswick, Georgia

Rossi and Prentiss had interviewed a number of employees at Clenteen Enterprises who'd worked with Lawrence Silvan and Jason Fryman ten years ago. They had learned very little.

Now they sat with Clenteen's human resources director, Dorothy Pilson, a middle-aged woman with gray-flecked brunette hair, who might have been someone's kindly aunt, albeit one who guarded information about her employees like a pit bull.

Rossi was getting fed up. "You know, Mrs. Pilson, this *is* a federal investigation."

She smiled as if trying to explain to a slow child. "Please understand my position, Agent Rossi. My job is to preserve the privacy of our employees, past and present."

"Understand *my* position," Rossi said. "We're trying to catch a murderer who has killed at least six teenage girls."

They endured a tense silence for a while. Next to Rossi, Prentiss sat quietly and, standing behind her, Carlyle might have been a statue.

"Fryman and Silvan," Rossi said, his voice neutral, if not calm. "When did they give notice?"

Mrs. Pilson eyed him suspiciously, as if Rossi were after valuable Clenteen company secrets. Finally, she glanced at a folder on her desk.

"Mr. Silvan," she said with exaggerated formality, "gave his notice in May and left in June. Mr. Fryman"—she indicated another folder—"left somewhat more abruptly. He gave notice on June tenth, and was gone on the seventeenth."

"Thank you," Rossi said. With a half smile, he said, "That wasn't so hard, was it?"

"Agent *Rossi*," Mrs. Pilson said, offended.

Rossi's cell phone rang, signaling the end of the round.

While Prentiss and Carlyle made polite good-byes to Mrs. Pilson, Rossi adjourned to the corridor to take the call from Hotchner, who briefed him on the changing situation in Minnesota. Rossi thanked God they'd packed their stuff, which was already in back of the Tahoe.

Soon, in the SUV—Carlyle speeding them north on I-95 to the Brunswick Golden Isles Airport, red lights flashing, siren wailing—Rossi filled Prentiss in.

"*Another* kidnapping?" she asked, eyes wide. "In less than twenty-four hours?"

"Hotch thinks the UnSubs are getting ready to bolt."

"What set them off?"

Frowning, Rossi said, "Us, probably."

"You think?"

"I think," Rossi said. "We're getting too close."

"If we're a stressor," Prentiss said, "maybe that will get him to make a mistake."

"Maybe."

"Skeptical?"

Rossi shrugged a shoulder. "He's been planning for this day. If we're right, and I'm pretty sure we are, this UnSub has been preparing for years, ever since he abducted the last of those girls. He knew this day was coming, just like it did a decade ago. That first time may have blindsided him, but he seems pretty ready this time around. If he's abducted two blonde girls matching the description of the previous abductees—and he's done it within twenty-four hours—what does that tell you?"

Unhesitatingly, Prentiss said, "He's been shopping for replacements."

"That's it," Rossi agreed. "He's been shopping— and what happened the last time he changed locations?"

"The third girl he picked up, he was already on the road."

Rossi nodded glumly.

Prentiss asked, "What did you tell Hotch about our meeting with the HR director at Clenteen?"

"Fryman and Silvan were considered professional but private by their fellow employees. Nobody remembers whether either man ever mentioned having children. Neither ever attended company functions outside of work, and neither hung out with other employees. 'He was a quiet loner that we never thought would hurt anyone. . . .'"

Like every neighbor on every cable news network who was stunned to find out Ted Bundy or the BTK killer was living next door.

Prentiss asked, "Is Hotchner picking up Fryman and Silvan?"

"Trying, but having a hard time finding either one."

"Hotch wasn't having them followed?"

"That's a sore point—seemed premature to him. Didn't want to tip his hand too much and he didn't trust the locals to tail them."

Prentiss said, "We're going back because we can be more help there now." It wasn't a question.

Rossi nodded. "With the UnSub maybe on the run, none of this down here is going to help fast enough. We need to get back and lend a hand. Maybe we can at least figure out which direction the UnSub's going."

"Five minutes," Carlyle said as he swung the wheel right and sped down the ramp at the airport exit of I-95.

In less than half an hour, they had parked, bade Carlyle a friendly farewell, loaded their gear onto the plane and were buckling their seat belts as the copilot closed and sealed the outer door. Moments later, they were in the air.

The Learjet was getting a lot of mileage on this trip. Rossi couldn't imagine the fuel bills, given the price of oil these days. This sure beat back when he and Gideon and Max Ryan and the rest had been forced to fly commercial—and coach at that.

After they'd been in the air awhile, Prentiss, at her laptop, turned to him. "Do you think he'll try to stay in the lumber industry?"

Though they didn't know which man was their UnSub, they felt certain the killer was one of the two foresters.

"He managed to do it last time," Rossi said. "No reason to think he's thinking different now—why?"

"I've been studying locations where lumbering is major enough to afford our man an opportunity."

"What have you found?"

"Where were the two recent kidnappings?"

"Hibbing and some little town . . . Co-something."

Prentiss brought up a map of Minnesota on her laptop and narrowed in around Bemidji. "Cohasset?" she asked.

"Yeah, that's it."

"Both east of Bemidji."

Rossi considered that. "Canada?"

Prentiss shrugged.

"What else is that direction? Is there an interstate?"

"I-35 in Duluth. That's southeast. If he gets to that, he could go most anywhere in the country."

"Both are possible," Rossi said. "So is the possibility he wants us to believe he's going east while he doubles back, and heads for Washington or Oregon or somewhere out that way."

"How do we narrow it down?"

"This guy is a planner. He probably doesn't go to the grocery store without researching all parameters. So, if you were planning on leaving, and just waiting for a wake-up call—what would *you* do?"

Sitting forward, Prentiss asked, "What if he was going to leave anyway, and our getting the case was just a coincidence?"

"You know I hate that word."

"Yes, but listen—ten years ago, he buried three girls, then kidnapped one."

Rossi nodded. "Because the flood washed the last body out into the open."

"What if he was planning on leaving anyway?"

"Go on."

"If he ran because of the body turning up, leaving 'abruptly' as Mrs. Pilson put it, then Jason Fryman is our best suspect. But what if he had already put in his notice, already made the plan to leave, and the body being discovered just sped up his departure?"

"Then," Rossi said, "we have a scenario very much like what's happening in Bemidji . . . and we have an UnSub with a plan—a plan that would include having a job lined up already."

"Yes," Prentiss said with a tight smile. "He had a job ready last time. That case would make *Lawrence Silvan* the better suspect."

"Yes it would, and I might know how to find out for sure." He got out his cell phone and punched a number on the speed dial. "Garcia?"

"Yes, sir."

"I'm going to give you two names. Can you tell

me if either one has been online trolling employment sites in the last several months?"

"That doesn't sound hard," she said.

And she was gone.

Bemidji, Minnesota

Going west on Third, he pulled up at the stop sign at Beltrami. On his right was the Trattoria Florentine, a fine Italian restaurant where he occasionally brought His Beloved. He rolled through the intersection, and drove slowly to the next corner, the next stop sign. As he slowed, he turned on his right blinker. The car almost seemed to be driving itself. He turned right onto Minnesota and drove north. He still had two blocks to turn away, but knew he wouldn't, the compulsion simply too strong.

It had started as he drove back into town, still behind the wheel of the rental car, the little girl still unconscious in the trunk. He passed the small businesses that made up the heart of downtown, glanced over as he drove by Celli's, an Irish bar and grill where he stopped for lunch now and then. Up ahead, like warriors lining a gantlet, were the redbrick buildings of the courthouse, jail, and law enforcement center.

He was going to drive right through the middle of them—and with the girl in back.

His Beloved might well send *him* to finishing school for such brazen foolishness. The thought gave him a perverse smile.

As he rolled up to the last stop sign, the court-house and jail across the intersection on his right, the law enforcement center on his left, he knew this was his last chance. His mind screamed, *"Turn!"* His gut said, *"No way."* He glanced over to where city patrol cars, the county's Durangos and, lately, the FBI's Tahoes were normally parked

They were gone now, out looking for him, no doubt. They would be sadly disappointed. Even more so, if they knew he was sitting at the corner, virtually right outside their front door. He stuck his tongue out. Childish, yes, but it gave him a warm glow and buoyed his courage.

"Heck with it," he said, and drove up the street, right between the very buildings where he would be spending most of the next year, if they caught him. After that, of course, it would be life behind bars in a federal prison—*if* they caught him. And, as far as he was concerned, that was a mighty big "if."

They would be on their way to his house by now, assuming they were any good, and he had a hunch that this team of federals was *very* good. Of course, he wasn't there. His Beloved wasn't home, either, already safely away with the other new member of their family. When the police got to the house, they would find it empty—stripped really.

Already vacated.

The police would, naturally, assume that he and His Beloved were already on the road with the two girls. Traveling would be next to impossible for the next few days. Still, all highways would be blocked, any cars checked that looked like his—only the car had been sold. When they did find it, the police would be very surprised. His new car was waiting at the motel, by the airport, as was His Beloved and their child.

The plan was that he would bring the brand-new girl to the motel, drop her off, and then he would help the girls nap again, so His Beloved could follow him to the airport to drop off the rental. While at the motel, he would change the license plates on the rental back to the originals.

Driving by the police department had been reckless, but he smiled as he turned north on Irvine Avenue. What was life without occasionally doing something just for fun? The police thought they were so smart, but he was so far ahead of them, he'd lapped them by now.

Law enforcement would be watching every interstate, two-lane highway, city street, and dirt road. The airport and the bus station would be covered. The law would be looking for him everywhere except right under their noses, which was where he was.

At the motel, a mom-and-pop place whose business was made up mostly of parents visiting their kids at Bemidji State, he backed the car into room 11's space, far enough from the office to be relatively secluded. At the door, he gave a single rap, to let His Beloved know who it was. Honey, I'm home!

She opened the door and smiled at him, so beautiful.

Despite the pressures they both were under, she could still smile at him; and Lawrence Silvan could not help but smile back. His wife, Suzanne, seemed to him as exquisite in her forties as she had at nineteen back in Ames, Iowa. Her brown hair was tied up in a loose bun, a blonde shock hanging down almost over an eye, Veronica Lake peekaboo style.

She was nearly as tall as Lawrence, her brown eyes wide-set and bright, her body lithe in tight jeans and an online-ordered T-shirt with the maroon and silver colors and logo of Washington State University, to help them fit in with their new surroundings.

He stepped inside and she kissed him lightly on the mouth.

"How'd it go?" she asked.

"Just fine, darling," he said. "She's gorgeous—you're going to love her."

Suzanne's grin revealed small, white, perfect teeth.

"What would you think," she said impishly, "about . . . Linda?"

They gave their girls new names as soon as possible, their own little christening service. Suzanne had decided she wanted L names this time around—Linda, Laura, Lucy. The girls who'd attended finishing school in Georgia had been Rs—Rose, Renee, and Rachel. The girls who went to finishing school in Minnesota had all had P names—Pam, Patty, and, of course, lovely Paula.

Suzanne looked over her shoulder at the small blonde girl tied to a chair, her mouth gagged, her cheeks and eyes red from crying, her blue eyes wide with terror.

"She's having a time-out," Suzanne said.

"Oh? Why?"

"For trying to scream."

"Well, maybe she'll feel better when she meets her sister."

"I can't wait," Suzanne said, eyes bright. "We've been so nervous all afternoon."

"I'll get her."

Suzanne held the door as he went and unlocked the car's truck. He held the lid unlatched but down as he watched the traffic passing on the street. When a break came, he let the lid up, swooped in, and picked up their new daughter—Linda—and rushed her into the room, settling her gently on the nearby bed. He glanced up to see little chair-bound Laura's eyes widen even more. She tried to scream through the washcloth gag, but nothing came out.

She would learn.

Lawrence went back outside, shut and locked the trunk, looked around one more time, then went back in and closed the door. Suzanne was already hovering over the new girl—his wife, Lawrence knew, was a born mother.

Suzanne brushed the hair of the unconscious girl;

then her shining eyes met Lawrence's adoring gaze. "Sweetheart, she's beautiful."

Pride warmed his heart. "I just knew you'd like her."

"No," she said, tears welling. "I *love* her."

Lawrence felt the glow that accompanied his wife's happiness. He had used a slow day at work last month, when it was still warm, to take a shopping trip to Crookston, west of here, just short of the North Dakota line. That pretty little girl would make their family complete.

Suzanne asked, "How long has she been sleeping?"

Lawrence glanced at his watch. "Oh, three hours the first time, an hour and a half this time."

"It took you two a long time to get back."

"I circled way south. I figured they wouldn't be looking for me down there. Took a little longer that way. Sorry, dear."

She gave him a peck on the cheek. "As long as you're both all right. I'll get my coat and we can take the car to the airport."

He touched her arm. "I've got to run one more errand before we do that."

She frowned. "What's that?"

"I've got a coat of Linda's. I want to put it in the trunk of the car we sold to Jason."

Her frown deepened. "Couldn't we just *go*?"

"No." Such moments required a rare firmness from him toward His Beloved. "We have a new life waiting in Tacoma. The only way we can live that

life, securely, is if someone takes the blame for"—
his eyes went to the two frightened little girls—
"sending the girls to finishing school."

"You *know* that was necessary."

"I do, darling. I do. But so is putting the blame
on Jason. Otherwise, they will track us down, and
once we're settled, it won't be hard to find us at all."

Her expression said she knew he was right, even
if she couldn't admit it out loud.

Lightly he said, "Anyway, Jason doesn't live that
far from here—should already be home from work.
Won't take long at all."

"All right, dear, but *hurry*, will you? I'm feeling
strangely . . . disconcerted."

"Don't be." He took his cell from his pocket and
showed it to her. "I'll call as soon as I'm on my
way back."

She kissed him, but worry tightened her lovely
eyes. "I have a terrible feeling of foreboding."

He hugged her. "Just nerves. I'll be back before
you know it."

And Lawrence went off to do this one last thing,
knowing another ten years of happiness awaited
him, and maybe this time, with the "L" girls, they
could be finished with finishing school.

That was his dream, anyway.

Bemidji, Minnesota

In the living room of Jason Fryman's home, Derek
Morgan stood at a window looking out on the street.

Behind him, Hotch and Reid were in chairs facing the sofa, where Fryman and his wife perched nervously. Garue stood next to Morgan, but with his attention on the couple.

The agents had already been to the Silvan residence and found no one home. They were in the process of trying to finesse a warrant to search the premises, but—in the meantime—they had come to interview the Frymans.

The thin blond Fryman, who'd been nervous in the interview room, was even jumpier now, a skittish pigeon flitting around his stoic, steady wife, Amy, a pretty, chubby, brown-eyed brunette. Fryman was in the same blue work shirt, jeans, and boots as in the interview room, while Amy Fryman wore a long, floral skirt, a brown blouse, and wire-frame bifocals—she seemed vaguely hippieish to Morgan.

The couple had been fully cooperative and Fryman had answered every question, the interview almost over now. When Morgan had interviewed Fryman before, the little man had seemed their best suspect. Now Morgan was convinced Silvan was the UnSub.

A blue Ford Taurus slowed in front of the Fryman house, the driver possibly looking in this direction, but in the gray of dusk, Morgan couldn't be sure. Then the car continued on.

Hotchner was saying, "So you have no plans for getting a new job out of state?"

"No," Fryman said, his voice small, wounded.

"You do know we'll check into this."

Mrs. Fryman said, fairly shrill, "We have done

nothing but cooperate. We've said you can search our home, top to bottom, without a warrant. What else do you want from us?''

Hotchner twitched a fairly ghastly smile. "We appreciate that. But we have to check every lead."

"There are no children here, there never have been any children!" She began to weep, then to sob.

Morgan was about to make sure the woman was all right when the corner of his eye caught the blue Taurus going by again, slowing as it went.

"Someone knows we're here," Morgan said, as the car pulled away again.

All eyes went to him.

"The same car has gone by twice," Morgan said, "once in each direction, and slowing down both times." He asked Fryman, "Do you know anyone with a blue Ford Taurus?"

The little man shook his head.

Hotchner asked Morgan, "What are you thinking?"

"Might be Lawrence Silvan."

Fryman, surprised, frowning, asked, "Why would *he* be here?"

Amy, through her sobbing, managed near hysterically, "Does he want to *kill* us?"

Silvan's name had come up enough in the questioning for the Frymans to figure out Jason's co-worker was a suspect.

Morgan held up a hand. "No, but if he's the guilty party, he's going to want to cover his tracks. He's got a new life set up somewhere. As close as we are, he's going to have to find a way to get us off his trail."

Reid said, "He'll try to frame someone."

"Could be," Morgan said.

Fryman was looking from agent to agent, tennis-match style. "What are you talking about?"

Ignoring Fryman, Hotchner said to the other profilers, "He knows we're closing in—he's a planner. He's always had a plan to cover his tracks in case of an emergency. He has to feed us someone who is a credible enough suspect that we'll leave him alone."

The Frymans looked absolutely perplexed.

"There's only one person that would fit that bill," Reid said, looking at Jason Fryman. "You."

Flummoxed, Fryman asked, "Why me?"

Still at the window, watching, Morgan said, "With the growing media attention, he's figured out we've tied these crimes to the ones in Georgia. Like they used to say in the old movies, he needs a patsy, a fall guy . . . and whoever he blames has to be someone who's here in Bemidji now, but who was also in Georgia at the time of the murders there."

Reid said, "Only two people that fit that bill, Mr. Fryman—Lawrence Silvan and you."

Fryman shook his head, eyes wild, a man trying to wake from a bad dream.

Hotchner got to his feet and pressed their host. "Has Silvan given you something lately?"

"No."

"Something just to . . . hold for him, maybe?"

Fryman shook his head. "Nothing." Then, frowning, he added, "Well . . . he did sell me his car. Real good price, too. Way under Blue Book. He said he was getting a new one to go with his new job."

The three agents traded looks.

"What?" Garue asked.

Reid said, "He's probably planted evidence."

Alarmed, Fryman blurted, "Of *what*?"

Hotchner said, "Something from the two recent kidnappings, most likely—*when* did you buy the car from him?"

"Not quite a week ago."

More to himself than Fryman, Hotchner said, "*Before* the kidnappings . . ."

The Fryman house was just beyond the city limits on a two-lane road with woods on either side and out back, too. That knowledge told Morgan what Silvan had been looking for.

"He was coming to plant the evidence now," Morgan said. "Only *we* were here."

Mrs. Fryman, more composed now but still afraid, asked, "Does that mean he's gone?"

From the window Morgan could see the woods on either side of the property, running almost to the road, framing the view. "Can he get into the woods in his car?"

"Oh yes," Fryman said. "There's a Bassinko service road less than a quarter mile that way."

He pointed in the direction the Taurus had disappeared.

Looking at Hotchner, Morgan said, "He's been planning this all along. The only thing that went

wrong was we were too quick, jumping on Mr. Fryman here as a suspect. For all the trouble we've been
having with this case, from Silvan's point of view?
We were actually *too* good."

Fryman asked, "*Now* what?"

Hotchner's eyes were on Morgan. "You have a
plan, don't you?"

Morgan nodded. "Mr. Fryman, does this house
have a basement?"

"Yeah, why?"

"Take your wife, and get down there now. Don't
come out until you hear us give an all-clear."

The Frymans rose off the couch and moved toward
the kitchen.

Hotchner asked, "Derek, what're you thinking?"

"Hotch, you have to leave."

That halted Fryman and his wife in their tracks,
and the husband blurted, "*What?*"

But Hotchner was on track with Morgan.

Reid was, too, and said, "He knows the FBI is here.
What he doesn't know is how many of us there are."

"Right," Morgan said. "Hotch, you, Reid and
Garue go. Silvan's going to hide in the woods until
he thinks the FBI has moved on—his whole new life
depends on his planting this evidence. If he fails, he's
had it. He *has* to do this. But he's not going to risk
it while the FBI is here."

Hotchner was nodding. "Mr. and Mrs. Fryman,
come back here, please—you need to walk us to the
door. When we leave, you get down into the basement, just as Agent Morgan said."

Fryman nodded. So did his wife.

Turning to Garue, Hotchner asked, "You familiar with this service road Mr. Fryman mentioned?"

"Sure."

"We'll pull out, and we'll go there. Then we'll come through the woods to back up Morgan."

"That," Garue said with a smile that cracked his leathery face, "is a plan."

While the others went out the front, performing their ruse, Morgan slipped out the back, leaving his parka behind despite the cold, moving along the old two-story house, his pistol in his hand, barrel down. He hugged the outer wall and hoped that Silvan had stayed in the woods on the east side, the direction Morgan had seen him take. The car Silvan had sold Fryman was parked nose-in in the gravel driveway on this side, in front of a freestanding two-car garage with its door down.

Morgan couldn't be sure from what direction Silvan might approach. His guess was the car would be the suspect's destination—that Silvan would be ready to plant something in the trunk, using a spare key he'd kept. That meant the UnSub's most likely avenue was not from behind the house, nor on its west, but on the east, where the car waited.

If Morgan was wrong, and Silvan came up in back, the profiler would make a good target should the UnSub have a gun. But if their profile was correct, Silvan would likely not be armed—this UnSub would do everything he could to avoid confrontation. A gun would hardly be this killer's first option. And even if Silvan did resort to a firearm, Morgan felt confident he'd be a hell of a lot more comfortable with his weapon than the other way round.

Still, lucky shots happened, and Morgan did not intend to be the victim of one. He slipped into the grassy space between the house and the garage and, at the front corner of the latter, peeked to see the SUV driving off.

The Frymans were not on the front porch. He hoped they were back inside and beating a hasty retreat for the basement about now.

The sun was almost down, the light fading fast. If Silvan didn't make his move soon, darkness might prevent Morgan from seeing the suspect until the guy got to the car. But Silvan had the other half of the same problem: Wait too long, and he'd be finding his way in darkness back to his own car.

The UnSub must have come to the same conclusion, because within moments Morgan saw the suspect slink out of the woods, in a Bassinko Company Windbreaker no less, moving low and slow across the yard, something in his hands—something made of cloth—his eyes glued to the front of the house . . . looking to see if Fryman might not come back out, Morgan realized, to put the car away in the garage.

The closer Silvan got, the faster the man moved, then made a sudden stop at the rear of the car. Morgan heard the click of a key in a lock. The trunk lid came up, blocking the suspect from the profiler's view.

Staying low, Morgan made the short distance to

the front of the car. They were at opposite ends of the vehicle now, each out of the other's sight. Morgan was low, next to a headlight, any slight sound he'd made having been covered by Silvan messing about in the trunk.

The killer was planting his evidence.

But to keep it from being too obvious, Silvan was burying it under the spare tire in the bottom of the trunk, from the sound of things, anyway.

When the trunk lid closed quietly, Morgan jack-in-the-boxed and pointed his gun across the length of the vehicle. "Freeze it right there!"

The bespectacled man couldn't have looked more stunned if Morgan had slapped him. The man's latex-gloved hands were on the trunk lid, and held no weapon.

The snout of his gun trained on Silvan's chest, Morgan said, "Lawrence Silvan, you're under—"

That was all he got out before Silvan bolted, sprinting for the woods.

"No!" Morgan yelled. *"Freeze!"*

Silvan kept running, Morgan in pursuit now, having been slowed a few seconds by navigating around the parked vehicle for the grass beyond the gravel.

On the run, the little man—*damn*, he was fast—fished something out of his pocket. Morgan thought it might be a gun, but it seemed too small for that, and anyway Silvan didn't raise his hand and aim whatever-it-was back at Morgan, whose own weapon was trained on the man, ready to shoot if Silvan gave him the slightest provocation.

As they neared the woods, Silvan kept going, his arms pumping, his head down. He was getting close to their darkening shelter when another voice yelled, *"Freeze!"*

Garue stepped from the edge of the forest, his gun trained on Silvan.

Who, finally, damnit, froze.

But he didn't entirely freeze, really, pressing a button on whatever was in his hand and bringing it up to his ear.

A cell phone!

"You were right, dear!" he said into it just as Morgan hit him with a flying tackle from behind. The phone went sailing into the trees as Silvan screamed, Morgan on top of him.

Morgan was cuffing and Mirandizing their suspect as Hotchner emerged from the woods with the cell phone in hand.

"He ended the call," Hotchner said.

"Where is she?" Morgan asked, jerking the cuffed Silvan to his feet.

"Who?"

"Your *wife*."

Silvan shrugged. "I don't know what you're talking about. I left something in my old car and just came around to get it."

"Wearing latex gloves?"

Silvan said nothing.

"Where are the girls you've abducted the last two days?"

"What girls?"

Reid was at Morgan's elbow. "He called his wife to warn her. She'll be on the run."

"We need to get Garcia on this," Hotchner said. "We need a new profile. This time for *Mrs.* Silvan."

Garue said, "I'll get an APB out," and moved away, getting on his own cell.

The forester's eyes were huge. "*I* did this, all right? But you need to know I was in this by myself. I killed them—killed them all. Suzanne had *nothing* to do with it. She doesn't even know the girls are dead. She didn't know they were stolen—she thought we were a foster home. This is *all* me."

As he led Silvan away, Morgan said, "You must be a hell of a forester, Silvan."

"What?"

"You sure know how to spread the fertilizer."

Darkness was on them now.

Chapter Eleven

Bemidji, Minnesota

In the interview room, Lawrence Silvan sat, small and smiling, across the table from SAC Aaron Hotchner. Uncuffed, the bespectacled man reminded Hotchner of a comic actor from his childhood television viewing, but he couldn't recall the name. Why did Silvan seem so smug, so pleased with himself, under these circumstances?

In front of Hotchner was a closed folder; his only goal in this session was to get those girls back, unharmed—nothing else mattered.

"Where are they, Lawrence?"

Silvan shrugged, his tiny smile ever present. This had been his response to every question he'd been asked since they were in the Frymans' yard and he'd blurted that absurd "confession."

Finally, in a small yet not really timid voice, the suspect spoke.

"I told you," Silvan said. Shrug, smile. "I killed them. I killed them all."

Wally Cox. That was the actor's name. Wally Cox.

"All right," Hotchner said, resigned.

The BAU team leader had hoped not to have the blatantly false confession as their starting point. Having to break that down, before getting to the truth, would cost time, and who knew how much time those girls had? How could they know Silvan's wife wouldn't dispose of the children on her way to disappear?

This was mitigated by Silvan knowing every bit as well as Hotchner that the forester would be spending the rest of his life in prison, without any possible hope of parole. This gave Hotchner absolutely nothing with which to bargain.

If the husband wanted to bear the entire weight of the crimes committed by him and his wife, Hotchner could do nothing to stop him, at least not with the evidence they had now.

"How did you kill them?"

Silvan eyed his inquisitor suspiciously. After a moment, he said, "I gave them an overdose."

"What of?"

"Of barbiturates."

"Where did you get the barbiturates?"

Again Silvan considered the question before answering. "I pilfered them."

"From where, Lawrence?"

"From my wife."

"Your wife uses barbiturates?"

"Suzanne has had trouble sleeping for a long time."

"Were these prescription medications, Lawrence?"

"Yes. Suzanne has needed sleeping pills and pain-killers for years."

"Why?"

"She had . . . problems."

"*Had* problems?"

"Had problems at home. When she was younger."

"What kind of problems, Lawrence?"

Silvan hesitated. "The emotional kind."

"And she got painkillers prescribed for her emotional problems?"

Silvan fussed with a shirt cuff.

"Do I have to repeat the question?"

Letting go of the cuff but not looking at Hotchner, Silvan said, "She got in trouble as a girl."

"Trouble."

"You know. As a girl."

"What kind of trouble, Lawrence?"

"Some boy got her in trouble."

"She was pregnant. Did she have the baby, Lawrence?"

This time the answer was prompt, with some old anger under it, the calm eyes flashing behind the glasses. "Some son of a bitch did it."

"Did what, Lawrence? Make her pregnant?"

"No! Gave her a bad abortion—when she was a teenager. That left her with chronic pain. Listen, I'm sorry."

"Sorry, Lawrence?"

"For swearing just then. I wasn't raised that way."

Hotchner paused at that speed bump. Then he asked, "And this . . . back-alley abortion, that's why Suzanne could never have children of her own?"

"Yes."

"That's very sad, Lawrence."

"I know." He was staring into nothing. "But I still wanted kids." The smug little smile returned. "So . . . I just took them when I saw one I liked. And made them mine."

"And Suzanne never knew?"

"Well . . . she, uh, because of her emotional problems, we couldn't, uh . . . adopt. That's why I told her we were going to be, you know, foster parents. She never knew how I got the girls. That was my little secret."

"She never wondered why no one official came around to talk to you and her about these foster children?"

"No. I said I handled all that."

"Why did you kill the girls when they got older, Lawrence?"

"They were nicer at a young age. Easier to handle."

"And Suzanne never suspected you were disposing of them when they reached a certain age."

"No. She just thought they'd been turned back over, to, uh, you know, the state or some agency. And that we'd been asked to be a foster home for a *new* batch of girls."

Then he smiled a little bit bigger. Hotchner knew why: The planner was improvising, and was proud of how well he was doing on the fly.

Hotchner decided to turn up the heat. "Did your wife know you were having sex with the girls?"

"I *wasn't!*"

Hotchner didn't think he was, but turned the knife,

anyway. "Isn't that why you had to dispose of them when they got older? They might tell your wife, or run and tell the authorities, what you were doing to them?"

The color drained from Silvan's face, his mouth yawning like a trapdoor. "I . . . I . . . would . . . would *never*. . . . do . . . such a . . . such a . . . *evil* thing. . . ."

Hotchner had heard many a killer speak of the world as seen through a distorted prism; but Silvan's definition of evil was brand-new even to the seasoned profiler.

"I would *never* harm those girls! I loved them . . . but not in a *sick* way."

"Until they became women. Once they reached puberty, you couldn't deal with them, could you? Or was it that as young women they were no longer physically attractive to you?"

"I never had relations with them—*ever*!" The UnSub who hated confrontation now had not a child to deal with, or even a teenage girl, but a grown man who was not having any of his lies. "I said before . . . I loved them. They were our children."

"They weren't your children, Lawrence; you abducted them. You stole them from their real parents. Why would you do such an evil thing if not to have sex with them?"

"It's not evil to want a family. It's not evil to take these innocent children to a safe place in a world this dangerous."

Hotchner wondered if the "safe place" was the Silvan home, or a hole in the ground; but this he did not ask. Not yet. "You and Suzanne wanted a family?"

"Yes," Silvan said, "but My Beloved had no part in how we . . . made that family."

"When you say 'we,' you mean you and your wife 'made' the family?"

"She raised the girls. She is a wonderful mother. But she would probably have been mad if she knew how I got the girls."

"Probably?"

"She'd have been angry with me."

"Angry for having relations with them?"

"I didn't! I told you, I would never do such an evil thing! We raised our daughters with love and care. You have scientists, don't you, who can look at the girls and tell that I didn't touch them? *Don't you?*"

Hotchner flipped open the folder, withdrew the pictures of the bodies and spread them before Silvan like a dreadful hand of cards. "You're right, Lawrence. The girls you loved and cared for were so decomposed that we couldn't tell if you had sexual relations with them or not."

Silvan took off his glasses, tossed them clatteringly on the table. Then his eyes went everywhere but at Hotchner or the photos—he'd glance down, then regard the ceiling, then study the walls, until finally he covered his eyes with his hands.

Silvan said, "You're not a good person."

"Oh?"

"What kind of person would show horrible pictures like that, of dead girls, to their father?"

Hotchner tapped one of the photos. "You see, Lawrence, since we couldn't tell through forensics, we just assumed you had sex with all six. That's what men who steal little girls do."

"*I* didn't," Silvan insisted, hands still shielding his eyes.

"*Look at them*," Hotchner said through his teeth. "They were beautiful young children, and you stole their childhood, and took their lives."

Silvan shook his head, eyes covered, moaning but saying nothing.

"*Look*, Lawrence! We'll sit here till you do."

Slowly, Silvan uncovered his eyes and they went to the photos. Without his glasses, the man might have seen only a blur of the decomposed horror; nonetheless, he lasted barely five seconds before turning away, and tears began to stream. Silvan looked like a child himself now—a small boy.

Hotchner knew that this man, in his own warped way, had indeed loved these girls. That didn't mean Silvan hadn't killed them, but this was likely the submissive half of the couple. The submissive would dispose of the bodies, but the dominant one would be the one doing the killing.

And Suzanne Silvan had the two little girls now. The only difference was that this time, the dominant partner might also have to dispose of the bodies.

Hotchner said, "You loved those girls." Not a question.

Silvan nodded meekly.

"And you didn't have sex with them."

Silvan whispered hoarsely, "I swear to the Lord I didn't."

"You also didn't kill them."

Silvan said nothing, his eyes closed, his breathing ragged.

Hotchner tapped a photo. "It tears you apart inside, seeing them like this."

". . . Yes."

"You and I both know there are two more girls out there who will meet the same fate unless we do something."

Silvan said nothing, but his eyes were still producing tears and his mouth was quivering.

"Lawrence, you need to tell me where Suzanne has taken them."

Silvan swallowed snot. Then he asked, "Why should I?"

"Why? So we can save them!"

"As long as I'm locked up," Silvan said, his voice peaceful, "they don't need saving. They'll grow up happy and loved."

"And then be murdered."

The smug little smile returned, though dripping with tears now. "No. You still don't understand. That's when they're *really* saved."

And Hotchner knew this man would never give up his "Beloved."

Then Silvan added, "Who knows? Maybe this time they won't have to go to finishing school."

"Finishing school?"

Silvan shrugged. "It's just a phrase."

But Hotchner knew at once. "A euphemism for killing the girls? Is *that* what she called it?"

Silvan was cleaning his glasses on his shirt. "No, it's *my* phrase—that's what *I* called it. Suzanne wasn't part of this, remember?"

Hotchner knew he was facing a dead end and was almost relieved when a knock came at the mirrored window.

When Hotchner exited the interview room, he left the pictures spread out on the table before Silvan, the little forester still doing his best not to look at them, but as if passing a car wreck, occasionally glancing anyway. Maybe a few minutes alone with the photos would change the man's attitude.

But Hotchner doubted it.

Morgan, who'd been in the observation booth, joined Hotchner in the hall.

"What?" Hotchner asked.

"We know where Suzanne Silvan is headed."

"Excellent. Garcia?"

Morgan flicked a smile. "Garcia. She did some digging when we started putting together Suzanne's profile. Her parents, Jacob and Tess Hamilton, have been dead for years. But they left her the family farm just outside of Ames, Iowa."

"Nice to know, but why do we think she's going there?"

"She kept the land, but in her maiden name. It would have been hard as hell for anyone to track."

"Unless they had Penelope Garcia doing the digging."

"Exactly."

"Okay, Suzanne owns land in Iowa—that still doesn't tell me why she's going there instead of anywhere else."

Morgan nodded. "Fair enough. Try this—she's never worked outside the home and has no education past high school. She may have some money they've saved, but what about when that runs out? Where better to get a job than somewhere where people already know her?"

Hotchner said, "And with the farm in her maiden name, no one will come looking for her there, or so she thinks."

"If Silvan was somehow able to escape, or wriggle out of this on a legal technicality, they have to have a backup in place."

"With a planner like Lawrence Silvan they would."

"Right. But how would he find her? He has to *know* where she's going . . . and with him in jail, it sure as hell isn't Tacoma. I think that family farm was the backup plan all along, a sort of safe house should they need it. After all, Lawrence is not the only one in the family who can plan."

"Why haven't they gone there before?"

"Haven't needed to. And that part of the country doesn't fit Lawrence's career needs."

Hotchner gave up a smile. "That's very good work, Morgan. How long will it take us to get there?"

"Oh, we're not going."

"Really," Hotchner said skeptically. "Were you promoted while I was in doing that interview?"

Morgan grinned. "Rossi and Prentiss were flying here to join us."

"Ah—and you diverted their plane."

"Yep. I think that's called taking initiative."

"It is, and you did well."

"Even if she drives straight through," Morgan said, still grinning, "Dave and Emily'll be waiting for her."

"*If* you're right about where they're heading."

Morgan's grin vanished, but something faintly kidding was in his reply: "Hotch, I'm a trained professional. You doubt my profile?"

Hotchner said nothing.

Fishing a bill from his pants pocket, Morgan said, "Twenty says Rossi and Prentiss get her at the farm."

Hotchner surrendered half a grin. "I know you're trained, Derek—I helped train you. You don't expect me to bet against myself, do you?"

Ames, Iowa

The sun peeked over the horizon as SSA David Rossi sat in the front seat of an unmarked car next to plainclothes investigator Tom Matcor from the Iowa State Patrol. Prentiss, in back, was trying with intermittent success to nap.

Knowing they had a head start, they had taken motel rooms to shower and change clothes, but had not taken the time to sleep. Instead, the two profilers had organized a plan with the help of the Iowa state troopers, and for almost two hours had been parked next to an outbuilding on the Hamilton family farm just west of Ames.

Mostly for communications purposes, patrol cars were stationed at the next farm in either direction; and, just in case, at a farm barely a quarter mile farther west of the Hamilton spread, a SWAT team waited.

Rossi, who hunted game, had achieved an almost Zen-like ability to remain patient—no point in wanting something to happen; you just had to wait and be ready. Either game would show itself or it wouldn't.

Another hour elapsed before a call came from the squad car to the east: *"Gray Toyota Camry with a temporary plate in the rear window just went by, headed your way."*

"Roger that," Matcor said into the handset.

Less than a minute later came the sound of a car heading up the gravel driveway. Prentiss sat up, wide-awake, alert. Rossi marveled at how she did that, and wished he could wake up that fast himself.

His voice low, Rossi said, "Patience . . ."

The house, a two-story clapboard, probably built in the 1930s, faced the road, its drive a long curling gravel path on the west. The unmarked sat just east of an outbuilding on the northwest corner of the house, separated by the gravel drive that went on up a short hill to a circle in front of a barn twenty yards farther east. The house blocked the vehicle on the south, the barn on the east and the outbuilding on the west.

Since the highway was south of the property, Suzanne Silvan would not be able to see them until pulling up the driveway near the back door of the house; and by then, when she saw them, it should be too late. . . .

As the car rolled into sight, Rossi—like Prentiss, in an FBI jacket—got out the passenger side into crisp coolness, keeping the car door open and between himself and his target; even though he considered the woman nonviolent, procedure was procedure. His pistol-in-hand hung loosely at his right side, its barrel pointed to the ground. Prentiss with Matcor was on the other side of the unmarked.

When Suzanne finally looked up and saw them in the dim light, she hit the brakes, then shifted into reverse. The state patrol cars came rolling up, however, one in the driveway behind her, the other having circled around the front, through the yard, and around to block her.

Over the top of the open car door, Rossi yelled, "FBI, Mrs. Silvan! Step out of the car with your hands up."

No movement in the vehicle.

Hadn't she heard him? The windows were up, the engine running. He was about to try again when the driver's-side door slowly opened and a slim, attractive woman—about five-seven, in jeans, a light jacket halfway unzipped revealing a maroon sweatshirt, and leather running shoes—slipped out, hands raised high.

"You folks have made a mistake," she said, her voice clear and loud. "My name is *Hamilton*."

Rossi came around and approached her.

The woman with her hands up had brown hair tied back in a loose ponytail, a comma of blonde hair hanging down near one eye. About a foot away, he stopped.

Staring into marble-hard brown eyes, he said, "Suzanne Hamilton *Silvan*, you mean. And the only one who's made a mistake is you. Turn around and assume the position."

The woman did as she was told.

As she leaned against the hood, Rossi pushed the power lock button on the open driver's-side armrest. The doors clicked and Prentiss opened the passenger back door, said something Rossi couldn't quite hear, then emerged with a little blonde girl in her arms. The child was crying, but appeared to be all right.

"It's okay," Prentiss cooed. Then, looking up at Rossi, she said, "Both girls are here—they seem to be fine."

"You be careful with my daughters," Suzanne said sharply.

"Stealing them," Rossi said coldly, "doesn't make them yours."

Over her shoulder, Suzanne did her best to look offended, and was fairly successful. "I'm no kidnapper."

"Maybe you aren't," Rossi said. "But your husband, Lawrence, is, and you're his accomplice after the fact and probably before."

"That's absurd."

"Murder, kidnapping, crossing state lines with those girls, are a lot of things, but absurd isn't one of them. You enjoy this sunrise—it'll be the last one you'll ever see outside prison walls."

Prentiss handed the first girl to a trooper, then the second one to another. The children were confused but neither was crying now; they seemed to sense they'd been rescued.

"Dave," Prentiss called, "they're going to be fine."

Rossi nodded. Coming around the car, Prentiss patted the woman down as Rossi, holstering his weapon, read Suzanne her rights.

"She's clean," Prentiss said, cuffing the woman, then turning her around.

Suzanne Silvan was sneering at Rossi, arrogant. "I hope you don't think I'm going to talk to you without a lawyer present."

"We can get you one here," Rossi said, "or where we're going."

"I'm in no hurry. I'll pick one eventually. You see, I think you're wrong—I think I'm going to see a lot more sunrises."

"Really?" Rossi said.

She laughed. "Do you really expect me to believe that Lawrence blamed *me* for all of this? *He's* the kidnapper, and knowing how weak he is, I'll just bet he's confessed."

"Oh, he has."

She smiled at Rossi in supreme self-satisfaction.

"Of course," Rossi said, "he didn't know we were going to catch you with the two children he kidnapped from Minnesota and you transported to Iowa, which I'm afraid does make you a kidnapper, too."

Her smile faded only slightly. "I can explain that."

So much for waiting to pick out a lawyer.

"Be my guest," Rossi said.

"Lawrence sent me here with the girls. He threatened to kill me and them if I didn't do as he said. I had to bring them here to protect them."

That didn't make much sense, which Rossi didn't bother pointing out. Instead, he asked, "So you were aware these girls had been kidnapped?"

She frowned.

"Lawrence said you thought all of the girls he's kidnapped over the years were foster children."

"Well . . . of course, I did." Her eyes danced. "But this time, he confessed what he'd been doing all this time. . . . You can't imagine how shocked I was to learn what had been *really* going on . . . and how foolish, how stupid it made me feel."

"You're right."

"What?"

"I can't imagine." Rossi smirked at her; couldn't help himself. "This happened before the call he made to you, I take it, right before he was arrested."

"Call?"

" 'You were right, dear'? Before you deny it, remember, there'll be cell phone records."

"Oh, *that* call," she said. She raised her chin, looked down her nose at him. "Why, that just sounded like gibberish on my end."

"Sounds like code for you to grab the girls and go."

Now it was her turn to smirk. "I'd like to see you try to prove that."

Rossi shook his head. "I probably won't bother. I can't prove my profile, either."

"Profile?"

"We're with the Behavioral Analysis Unit. It's our job to profile the killer . . . and I was sure it was *you*, not Lawrence."

"I didn't even know the girls were dead! Lawrence said he'd sent them back to the state authorities. That our foster care was over."

"Why, because it was time for them to go to 'finishing school'?"

That took the smile off her face. That told Suzanne Silvan that hubby Lawrence had opened up to his interrogators, at least to some degree.

"How did you manage it, Suzanne? How did you get Lawrence to shoulder all of the blame? He must love you very much."

"He does. He's my husband."

Ross pretended to chuckle. "I mean, I understand the brainwashing—you've had twenty-five years to work on him. You were able to convince him to acquire a family for you, one little blonde abductee at a time. Then, even after you raised the girls together, when they got to that difficult age? You even convinced him it was normal, it was right, it was all part of your loving marriage, for him to dispose of the bodies of the 'daughters' you'd killed."

"I didn't kill anyone. I told you, I didn't know they were dead. It's a tragedy."

"Yet you seem to be over it already." Rossi grunted a laugh. "And then you somehow got him to start the cycle all over again, got him to go along with you on a second round of kidnapping and family life and then murder . . . but the third time really wasn't the charm, was it?"

Her chin was up again, but nothing like a smile was anywhere on her face. "One man's opinion," she said.

"Actually, my whole team's opinion, six of the top criminal profilers in the world."

She summoned another sneer, a little one. "Six expert opinions against those of twelve licensed drivers. And how do you think that will come out?"

Shrugging, Rossi said, "You're probably right, they'll believe Lawrence. God knows when I heard the tape of his confession, I believed it. How he abducted each girl, how he brought them home, how he killed each one with pills he pilfered from you, how he dressed them, protected them with the blankets and plastic before he buried them."

Suzanne Silvan's self-satisfied expression returned—a multiple murderer convinced she would get away with her crimes.

Rossi was out on a limb now; he was bluffing his ass off. He had in fact not heard a tape of the confession and only had received a brief summary from Hotch on the phone; but he knew the profiles of Lawrence and Suzanne Silvan, and he knew how this woman thought.

They were standing in this yard on this crisp, beautiful morning because twenty-five or so years ago, this twisted woman had been an innocent herself, abused by her father and unprotected by her mother. Sick as it was, she actually thought she was protecting "her" girls from such a fate. Starting their periods had signaled the end for these girls, as otherwise they would become women and enter a corrupt world, a world so perverse and cruel that Suzanne—scarred by her childhood—felt that only by killing them could she save them.

Then a thought flashed through Rossi's mind: Maybe it wasn't the world outside she was protecting them from, not entirely; maybe she wanted to remove them from the presence of their "father"—the adult man of the house, Lawrence Silvan.

"Yep, Lawrence told us everything he did," Rossi said. "He claimed the thing he was most ashamed of was having sexual relations with the girls."

Suzanne's eyes widened and her mouth dropped open.

Rossi had hit the hot spot and—for a long moment—he could practically see the wheels turning as she tried to come to grips with what he was saying . . . and was he telling the truth?

"Each seduction in detail," Rossi said, and shuddered. "Horrible to hear. He said he was always telling you how much he loved the girls . . . sort of a veiled confession, I suppose . . . and yet you never caught on. Of course, he was so fearful of what you might do, a veiled confession was as close as he could bring himself."

Her eyes were darting, her mind racing.

Then he remembered how she'd reacted when he used the phrase "finishing school"—Morgan had told him about that on the phone, Silvan using that odd phrase as a euphemism for murder.

"I wonder," Rossi said, "if you know what sending the girls to 'finishing school' meant to Lawrence?"

Her features tightened.

"He told us that to him, having sexual relations with them, that was 'finishing school.' He said, as soon as the girls began to 'blossom,' he began to have relations with them."

"No!"

"He said he didn't want them to die without knowing the real joy of being a woman."

"No, no, no!"

"He said for several months before 'he' killed each girl—and, of course, we know who *really* killed the girls, don't we, Suzanne?—he made sure they knew the real happiness of experiencing a man's touch. He didn't want them to die without that knowledge."

"I . . . I failed them. . . ." Tears were streaming now; lips quivering. She fell back against the car. "You have to believe me, I didn't know he was doing that! I'd *kill* him if he were here. I swear I'd kill that little dried-up son of a bitch. . . ."

"How did you fail them, Suzanne?"

"I thought I'd saved them, all of them—Rose, Renee, Rachel, Pam, Patty, little Paula—but I failed them all, didn't I?"

"Did you?"

"You have to believe me—I *tried* to save them. Lawrence didn't put the girls to sleep—*I* did. I gave them their medicine, their overdoses, to spare them. You have to understand, once I began having my monthly 'friend,' my father would spend more nights in my room than in his and Mother's. And when I tried to get Mother to help, she wouldn't. She pretended not to believe me, and I swore I'd never be a terrible mother like her. *Never.*"

Rossi glanced at Prentiss, who was standing mute witness to this entire exchange.

"Oh, she did one thing for me, my mother—she got my tubes tied, so my father couldn't make me pregnant again. That was how she chose to deal with him pawing at me, sticking that . . . that *thing* in me." The whites of her eyes showed all round, and her voice became shrill. *"Not* my girls. That would never happen to *my* girls. I knew all men were alike, even Lawrence—but I thought if I got the girls out of the house when their monthly friend came, I thought . . . I thought . . . well, I *never* thought that Lawrence would do that to them, when they were just innocent little girls!"

"You had to be cruel to be kind," Rossi said. "Kill them to save them."

She nodded. "I sent them to finishing school—

that's what that phrase was supposed to signify. They were meant to go to heaven pure, innocent, unde-filed."

While she was talkative, Rossi decided to dot the i's and cross the t's. "Since you couldn't have chil-dren of your own, you talked Lawrence into kidnap-ping little girls for you."

"Of course." She gazed at him in shock that he just didn't seem to get it. "*All* normal people want to have a nice family."

What could he say to that? Maybe that the finish-ing school Suzanne Silvan was likely to attend would be a lethal-injection chamber.

To a nearby trooper, Rossi said, "Take her."

The trooper guided her by the elbow to a squad car.

Rossi had only one thing left to say: "Suzanne?"

She looked back at him through tear-filled eyes.

"There is one thing you should know."

"Yes?"

"Lawrence never said any of those things I said. He would have gone to Death Row for you."

Her expression turned quizzical. "Then why . . . why did you say those terrible things?" She shook her head. "Just like a man . . . just like a man . . ."

Prentiss was at his side. "I got it all," she said, and held up the little recorder. "That was good work."

He grunted. "Yeah. Me and her father."

Rossi walked to the farmhouse and sat on a front step. He felt like he could sleep for a hundred years. They had saved two little girls, and would return them (if traumatized) to their families; but Rossi still felt lousy about this one.

For over twenty years these people had ruined the lives of six girls and their families, and damaged another two families in recent days. They had been damned lucky to even identify the last three—Rossi figured they owed that mostly to advances in DNA matching. The other three, the ones buried in the woods in Georgia? It would take a miracle to pinpoint the parents of those girls.

When they got back to Quantico, Rossi would make a point of trying to track the Silvans' movements immediately after their marriage; Reid would help, and so would Garcia—if they had a miracle worker on the team, she was it—but he knew the odds against finding the parents of girls who disappeared somewhere in the United States in the early to mid-eighties.

Literally hundreds of girls would have gone missing back then. There weren't even AMBER Alerts; kids could vanish a lot more easily. He wasn't confident, but they had to try.

That was the job, and he was fine with it.

What he could not fathom, what he could not begin to understand, in all his profiling expertise, was why he felt such a hollow victory over what he'd done.

And why he found himself feeling pity for the monster that a little girl named Suzanne Hamilton had become.